no. 2

# of heroes and villains

mark delaney

PEACHTREE

ATLANTA

To Mom and Dad
who, after raising eight children,
have earned their own capes and tights.

A FREESTONE PUBLICATION

Published by
PEACHTREE PUBLISHERS LTD.
494 Armour Circle NE
Atlanta, Georgia 30324

www.peachtree-online.com

Text © 1999 by Mark Delaney
Cover photograph of film reel © 1999 by Eyewire

Scream 2 © 1998 Dimension Films. All rights reserved.

Star Wars, The Empire Strikes Back, Millennium Falcon, Darth Vader, Luke Skywalker, Yoda, lightsaber, and stormtrooper are registered trademarks of Lucasfilm Ltd.

Godzilla is a registered trademark of Toho Co., Ltd.

X-O Manowar © 1996 by Acclaim Comics Inc., a division and registered trademark of Acclaim Entertainment, Inc.

Batman and Swamp Thing are registered trademarks of DC Comics, Inc.

Star Trek and Klingon are registered trademarks of Paramount Pictures

Book and cover design by Loraine M. Balcsik
Composition by Melanie M. McMahon

Manufactured in the United States of America

10 9 8 7 6 5 4 3 2 1
First Edition

Library of Congress Cataloging-in-Publication Data

Delaney, Mark
    Of heroes and villains / Mark Delaney. —1st ed.
        p. cm. — (Misfits ; #2)
        Summary: While the Misfits are attending a comic book convention and waiting for a sneak preview of the new Hyperman movie, they see the film stolen by someone dressed as Hyperman's nemesis, the Jester.
        ISBN 1-56145-178-9
        [1. Cartoons and comics—Collectors and collecting—Fiction. 2. Mystery and detective stories.]
        I. Title. II. Series: Delaney, Mark. Misfits ; #2.
    PZ7.D3731850f 1999
    [Fic]—dc21   98-36466
                                                   CIP
                                                   AC

table of contents

Acknowledgments

Special thanks to:
Lota Hadley
and others at Warner Bros. Studios Video Transfer Lab
for giving me the inside scoop on Telecine machines
and the magic of converting film to video

Bob Kane
1915–1998
Creator of Batman
for giving me the thrill to begin with

Dave Smith of Fantasy Illustrated
who's done more conventions, answered more of my
trivia questions, and listened to more of my comic
book prattle than any man alive...

Except my brother.

Prologue

Oh, how he hated the name Chuck.

Charles Leach sat at his office computer and banged out this week's edition of *Chuck's Soapbox,* a weekly column that appeared in every new release from Mercenary Comics. A month ago the column's title was *Stan's Insider,* but Stan, Charles's boss, had gotten tired of writing the stupid thing and had assigned Charles to take over. "Keep it light, but clever," Stan had said. "Talk up the new comics. Say cool things about Psychoblade and Razorclaw." It was Stan who had insisted on the hated nickname. "No, no, 'Charles' is all wrong. It's too smooth, too formal," he had said, drawing out the name, "Chaaarrrles," to emphasize the effect. "But 'Chuck' is catchy and fun. That's what I want from you, Chuck, *fun.*"

Charles paused in his writing and stared at his office wall, where a poster for the upcoming Razorclaw one-shot hung. It showed Razorclaw's severed head spiked on the Ocean King's royal trident (with the title

"Heads—You Lose!"). Being assistant editor at the hottest new comic book company in the business at least meant his work area *looked* interesting. On his desk was a cold-cast porcelain statue of Gridlock, the urban super-hero who pounded drug dealers by night and who, by day, was a Grammy Award–winning rap artist. On his bookshelf was a model of Psychoblade, in her leather bikini and bronze gauntlets, waving her fluorescent green energy sword.

To think that he would end up in such a place! Charles had a masters degree in comparative literature from a small but highly prestigious university. He should be at Random House, Simon & Schuster, or HarperCollins editing thick, epic romances or high-tech thrillers, nursing the powerful yet frail egos of best-selling authors. Here at Mercenary—the only place he had been able to find a job (there were too many idealistic English majors out there with the same fantasies he had)— Charles's dreams had languished.

At first the job at Mercenary Comics had seemed promising. A handful of the most popular artists from the major comic companies had banded together to start their own independent publishing house. The new venture had been the talk of the industry, a revolution. Only later had Charles realized that although the artists could draw spectacular images and eye-catching, action-packed, full-page panels, not one of them had the writing skills of an armadillo. So while other comic companies published some truly meaningful pieces of literature, their editors' offices decorated with Eagle and Eisner awards, Mercenary Comics had captured the market in sex, violence, and adolescent male power fantasies.

Worse, this headstrong group of artists had fought Charles at every turn. Charles had suggested many more literate, more *deserving* projects than the endless stream of nonsense offered up week after week by his creative teams. Their ideas never changed: "muscular brute *A* meets muscular brute *B,* and the two of them beat the royal snot out of each other." Charles nearly chewed his tongue off in story meetings, biting it so as not to insult the sensitive artists who signed his paycheck every other week. But he could not hold back the vague grumbles that escaped his lips from time to time. Though Charles had worked toward a full editorial position, he remained, after five years, an assistant editor. He sat in his office each day steaming while a series of younger, less-experienced hacks waltzed by his door on their way to their larger offices and fatter paychecks.

But no more. His dignity had suffered enough.

Soon, he thought, *very soon, I'll have more than enough money to quit this job. Go back to school. Earn my Ph.D. I'll be a professor, teach fine literature. I'll write novels and live in a large, colonial house in Connecticut—no, Vermont.*

At this thought, Charles's flash of temper left him. He smiled and closed his eyes, envisioning his new life. A moment later, when the phone jangled him from his

4   daydream, he sat up quickly and nearly dropped the receiver when he grabbed it.

"Charles Leach."

"It's all set," said the voice on the line. Charles immediately recognized the slow speech and whiny tone. He shuddered. An office assistant walking by happened to glance at him, and he nudged his door shut with his foot. "I thought I told you not to call me at the office," he hissed into the receiver. "In fact, I thought I said not to *ever* call me."

"Well, you wanted a report," the voice whined. "I'm giving you one."

Charles tapped his finger against his desktop until his anger faded. "All right," he finally said. "Give it to me."

"I got the job. These places are always willing to take on a 'helpful volunteer,' know what I mean? Everything is in place."

"And our assistant?"

"Oh, yes. Our friend had some reservations, but I think I took care of them. There won't be any problem."

"Good," Charles said. "I want this to go off without a hitch."

He hung up the phone and leaned back in his chair again, reveling in his hatred of Mercenary Comics and all it stood for. He stared at Psychoblade, conquering an urge to grab the hand-painted resin model and throw it against his office wall. "Chuck" *that*, Stan!

No, calm down, everything is all right, he told himself. *The plan will work. It has to.* Like everything else Charles controlled, the plan was neat and clean.

He allowed himself a smile, which lingered even as he turned to finish the ridiculous *Chuck's Soapbox.* Soon, some wonderful things would be happening: The comic business he loathed would pay his way through school, and then some. American Comics, Mercenary's rival in the market, would be in a tizzy, and the people of Bugle Point would see a comic book convention unlike *anything* they had ever seen before.

chapter
one

eugenia "Byte" Salzmann stood in line at the cafeteria and ran her fingers through her long, straggly hair. She told herself a thousand times she would never again forget to set her alarm clock. This morning she had overslept. Oversleeping meant she had to rush to get ready for school, rushing meant she did not have time to pack a lunch, and failing to pack a lunch meant eating in the Bugle Point High School cafeteria with hundreds of her peers.

That was the problem, of course—all the people. In all her years of school, Byte had never quite gotten used to being around so many people. And all of them so much alike—eating the same fast food, wearing the same designer labels, listening to the same music, using the same expressions—thousands of teen drones.

Byte paused in the long, cramped line of people. The bodies of other students closed in on her. She tried to will herself to move forward but couldn't. People began brushing past her, and Byte squeezed her shoulders together, as though she could make herself smaller by folding up her bones.

The people behind her pressed ahead, urging her forward. Arms reached for snacks off the chip rack, one after another, like arms on a factory robot. They were all parts of one huge lunch machine: Grab the plate. Get the burger. Fill the cup. Eat the chips. Don't forget the Coconut Sno-ball. That'll be $2.25. *Ka-ching!* Next!

Byte couldn't take it.

Instead of ordering, she left the line and bolted for the exit. The black nylon bag containing her notebook computer banged against her leg as she ran. The funny thing was, the whole time she was running her mind was telling her that normal people do not flee from a lunch line; normal people just absorb the sights and sounds and smells without any ill effects. But to Byte's senses, they were like a heavy blanket, smothering.

Once outside, a chilly wind tousled her hair and the sun warmed her face. She stood on the grassy area between the courtyard and the asphalt blacktop, and the world felt fresher and more open. Byte touched her hand to the pocket of her jeans. She felt the money folded there. This whole situation was so ridiculous! For a few moments, Byte just stood there. There was no one else around. The cold wind was invigorating, and she began to think more clearly. Then she began to smile.

She had an idea. She knew it would work, as long as Mrs. Langley gave permission.

8   Byte clasped her computer bag a little more firmly and began walking toward the school library. Mrs. Langley was busy at the library entrance, preparing the student bulletin board, and Byte watched for a moment as the librarian used a stapler to tack up a newspaper article about last night's basketball game.

"Oh…hello, Byte," Mrs. Langley mumbled. She had a pencil in her mouth. Mrs. Langley wrote notes to herself constantly, and she often kept a pencil or pen in her mouth as she worked.

"Hi, Mrs. Langley."

"What can I do for you, Byte?"

The librarian brushed her palms against her skirt and walked behind her desk. She always walked so quickly, Byte thought, as though getting that stapler or paper clip was an emergency medical procedure.

Byte crinkled her nose, a habit she had developed to keep her wire-framed granny glasses from slipping. She smiled and leaned against the edge of Mrs. Langley's desk. "I have a favor to ask," she said. "Remember a couple of months ago, when I forgot to bring my lunch?"

Mrs. Langley pursed her lips and nodded. She seemed to know what was coming.

"Well," said Byte, "I was kind of wondering if maybe I could do that again."

The librarian raised her pencil and began tapping it against her lips. She did not take long to make decisions. "Same rules as before," she said. "You share with the other fifth-period library aides, and no you-know-whats. Got it?"

Byte nodded. Mrs. Langley reached for the telephone and slid it in Byte's direction.

Byte pulled out her computer and turned it on. She unplugged the cord from the back of the phone, slipped it into the modem jack on her computer, and began tapping the keys. In seconds she had logged on with her online provider, worked her way onto the World Wide Web, and typed in the code for the Website she needed. There it was. Byte coded in her order, typed in the school's address and zip code, then logged off. She smiled at herself when she finished. Any kid could walk into a school cafeteria, plunk down a couple of bucks, and walk out with a hot dog and Tater Tots. But how many could order a pizza through the Internet and have it delivered to school during library period?

She had even remembered to leave off the "you-know-whats." Mrs. Langley *hated* onions on her pizza.

Byte felt a hand on her shoulder, and she turned to see Mrs. Langley standing beside her. The librarian sat down and gestured to a chair that was facing her. Byte sat.

"You know, Byte," she said, "you are a very intelligent, very talented young lady. But one of these days you're just going to have learn how to deal a little bit better with *people.*"

Byte looked at her hands in her lap and nodded. "I know," she said.

10 Mrs. Langley folded her arms. "You can't avoid everyone in the world, you know," she said. "We outnumber you."

"I'll try to do better," Byte said. "Starting tomorrow. I promise." She rose, plugged the cord back into the telephone, and closed down her computer, smiling.

She lifted her computer, and as she tried to slip it back into its nylon bag, she noticed something. Tucked into the bag's outer pocket was a small envelope. Byte took it out to look at it more closely and was not the least bit surprised to see that it had a tiny emblem scrawled on the outside: a circle superimposed over a square. Peter's emblem, the sign of the Misfits. Mattie Ramiro, that little phantom, must have somehow yet again slipped a note from Peter into her bag.

She opened the envelope and examined its contents. *What is this?* It was not a note after all—it wasn't even Peter's handwriting. It was a badge of some kind, a plastic card with a safety pin on the back. Strange writing and a drawing of a comic book character marked the front of it.

This is interesting, Byte thought. *What is Mattie getting us into now?*

Jake Armstrong sat in his second-period jazz band class and grimaced. He squirmed in his chair—which was much too small for his large frame—and studied the line of music again, those awful sixteenth notes with the syncopated punches. Fumbling with his clarinet, he concentrated on hearing the piece in his mind—the bright, bouncy "In the Mood"—remembering the recording of it that Mr. Janson, the band director, had just played.

He could feel it and play it—he knew he could—if he'd just relax and let himself. "Quit thinking and let the fingers work," Mr. Janson would say.

Last year, when he had made it into the city jazz band, Jake had come to realize that his music was more than a mere activity, more than a hobby. The night he had played at the summer festival, the audience cheering at "'S Wonderful" and "Puttin' on the Ritz," Jake had felt the music welling up from inside him—the vibrations not only in his clarinet, but in his bones. Never before had he felt such a crystallized sense of *This is who I am; this is what I do.* Jake had already decided where he wanted to go to college. Berklee College of Music. One of the most prestigious private music universities in the country.

But to accomplish that goal, he would have to be better than he was now. He would have to be the best. And he could start by mastering these stupid sixteenth notes.

Mr. Janson tapped his baton—*a-one, two, three!*—and the band began to play. Jake gazed at the music one last time, then closed his eyes, allowing his fingers to play from memory. Instead of forcing out the notes, trying to control them through sheer determination, he thought of the music as something like a river, a natural force

12 that moved all by itself and only happened to carry him along. Letting go, he played differently now, his fingers popping off the keys in perfect sync with the song's blistering rhythm. Mastering this piece was another step, he thought—like when he switched from a number three-and-a-half reed to a number four. The playing was more difficult, but his technical skills were getting better—a little better all the time.

Jake's mind wandered for a moment. He noticed something out of the corner of his eye: a small envelope lying in his open clarinet case. The envelope bore no name, but someone had scribbled a familiar emblem on the front: a circle intersecting a square. The emblem, Jake knew, was meant to suggest two things that would never fit together—a square peg and a round hole. It was the sign of the Misfits.

Byte Salzmann, Peter Braddock, and Jake Armstrong had met at the beginning of their freshman year and called themselves the Misfits. At the time, their friendship seemed a matter of desperation. Byte, at her mother's forceful prodding, had tried out for the school play and barely survived the humiliation. Peter had joined nearly every academic club on campus—and was intent on sharing his wisdom and advice on all club matters—but then was mystified when other club members began to drop out one by one until Peter stopped attending the meetings. Jake, in a burst of ninth-grade ambition, had tried out for football but failed to make the team—in spite of his muscular, six-foot-two, two-hundred-pound frame. His coach never understood how a player of Jake's size, speed, and sheer athletic grace could be so lacking in aggression. His teammates had been even less understanding.

Later Mattie Ramiro had joined the group. Hungry for acceptance, he had become something of a sidekick to Peter. Together, the four friends evolved into the group Misfits, Inc.

When band class was over, Jake picked up the envelope. Inside was a badge of some kind, a plastic card with a safety pin on the back. A crude drawing of a comic book character marked the front.

Jake studied the card, smiling. *Cool,* he thought. *Now how did Mattie pull this off?*

"Class," said Mrs. Scapelli, "today we'll continue our unit on debate. I'll assign topics and partners."

Peter Braddock groaned inwardly. Two months ago, Mrs. Scapelli, the speech and drama teacher, had attended a workshop on "Group Learning in the Classroom." Although Peter didn't know this for a fact, he was confident in his guess. Mrs. Scapelli had missed two days of class back in early December, and when she returned she suddenly knew thirty-seven different ways of forming random learning groups. Sometimes she drew from a deck of playing cards; sometimes she passed out slips of paper with numbers on them; and sometimes she asked students to choose color-coded plastic chips.

14   The method didn't matter. Peter Braddock *hated* learning groups.

The problem with learning groups was that one person in the group was generally, and often noticeably, smarter than the others. In this system, the less intelligent members of the group received a wonderful learning experience. The lazy members of the group found that the more dedicated students would actually do their work for them. And the smartest member of the group—well, the smartest member just got shafted, having the duty of carrying the others while trying to ensure that his or her own score did not suffer.

At least today, Peter thought, *I'll be working with a single partner instead of an entire group. I won't have to carry three people on my shoulders.*

"These color-coded envelopes will tell you which side of the debate question you will argue, affirmative or negative," said Mrs. Scapelli. "The question itself is sealed *inside* the envelope, so do not open it until I tell you."

Peter's envelope was green. On the outside of it, lettered in Magic Marker, was the word Affirmative. Someone else in this room, Peter's new partner, held a similar envelope. More importantly, his envelope also bore a tiny number 1 in the corner, indicating that Peter and his partner would be going *first*.

"Now, find your partner," said Mrs. Scapelli, gesturing broadly across the room and smiling as though she had just set free a flock of doves.

Peter remained in his seat. While others wandered the room, he held his envelope up where everyone could see it. Students milled all around him, located their partners, and slid desks together.

The air in the room was an odd mix of terror and laziness. January—and with it the first semester of the school year—was coming to an end. The speech class had completed its semester final last week; now the students were running through informal debates, a sort of tryout for the after-school debate squad.

Just then another green envelope landed on his desk with a loud *thwap*. Peter looked up and found himself staring into the one face he had least hoped to see. Robin Sutter stood above him, her arms braced against his desktop like a pair of steel girders. This was the Robin Peter knew at her most intimidating, the in-your-face Robin: blue eyes, auburn curls, one eyebrow raised in challenge.

Oh no, he thought, not even trying to hide his dismay.

"That's right," she said, "and don't think I'm any happier about this than you are." She grabbed an empty desk and scooted it next to Peter's. "So we're stuck with each other for the next fifty minutes. We'll survive. Who are we debating against?"

Peter looked around the room for another pair of green envelopes. These would bear the word Negative, and whoever held them would be Peter and Robin's opponents in the debate.

16   "There," said Peter. He nodded toward a corner of the room where a tiny girl with white-blond hair gripped a tell-tale green envelope. She wore a B.P.H.S. activity sweater with a brass math club pin. Her partner, a basketball player sporting a letter jacket and a buzz-style haircut, leaned back in his chair and made little dancing motions with his head, as though listening to music only he could hear.

Robin Sutter took one look at them. "They're toast," she said.

"You may now open your envelopes," said Mrs. Scapelli.

Peter and Robin opened their respective envelopes and removed the three-by-five-inch index cards tucked inside. Peter turned his card over and read aloud the typed statement.

"Resolved: that all high school students should be required to wear school uniforms."

"It's a slam dunk," said Robin. "The way I see it, I'll take the first affirmative, define the terms of the debate, and establish the foundation of our argument. You'll take the second, build on my points, and attack the negative points."

"Well now, wait a minute," said Peter. "I think maybe I should take the first shot."

Robin leaned back in her seat and gazed momentarily at the ceiling, as though she were a parent framing a response to a confused child. "No, Braddock," she said. "If you think I'm going to follow you just to clean up the mess you make, you're crazy."

Peter remained silent, backing off from the battle line to let Robin think through her position. He could tell she was doing that now by the way she studied the ink marks and scratches on her desktop.

"Okay," she said finally, "Maybe it wouldn't mess things up too badly if you went first." She looked up at him, and, as often happened when she rethought her brash behavior, her features softened.

"I just thought," Peter said, "that since you stayed up really late last night, you might find building on my points as *second* affirmative a little easier."

Robin shook her head, her false smile clearly masking some new-found anger. "I've known you since sixth grade, Braddock," she said. "Don't do that to me."

"What?" asked Peter.

"You know! That—that thing you do! That mind-reading game. It's freaky. And don't bother telling me how you knew I stayed up late. I know there's some really simple, stupid explanation that I should be able to see, and if you wave that explanation under my nose you'll just tick me off."

To preserve peace, they agreed that Robin would take the first affirmative argument and Peter the second. And twenty minutes later, the little blond girl and the basketball player were indeed toast.

When the bell rang ending the period, Peter gathered up his jacket, which he had slung over the back of his chair, and was surprised to find another envelope sticking halfway out of the pocket. Peter started to reach for it when someone sidled up next to him and lightly touched his shoulder.

"Hey, Braddock." Robin Sutter positioned herself between Peter and the classroom door. She faced him, smiling, her arms crossed in what Peter read as an unconscious gesture of self-protection. "Good job," she said. "And you would have been great going first, too."

Peter narrowed his eyes. "What are you up to?" he asked suspiciously.

She pointed to herself in feigned surprise. "*Moi?*" Then she headed out the door, waggling her fingers at him in more of a toodle-oo than a good-bye. ·

Peter finished pulling on his jacket and reached for the envelope. It was plain white, but it was made of a heavy, high-quality paper. His name was scrawled across it in scraggly handwriting. Above his name was a somewhat inaccurate re-creation of the emblem for Misfits, Inc., Peter's group.

He tore the envelope open, and a plastic card slipped into his hand. Peter saw the illustration on the card and the lettering below the illustration. Immediately realizing what the card was, he tapped it against his open palm, wondering how it had come to be in his coat pocket. *Mattie?* He was the most likely suspect in a case like this, but Peter discarded the idea. *No. Mattie couldn't afford this, it isn't his writing on the envelope, and the manner of delivery—well, it's just a little too obvious to be his work.*

Then someone in the almost empty room called his name. "Peter!"

He turned to see Mrs. Scapelli standing by her desk, grinning. "Great debate today," she said, "don't you think?"

"What? Oh…oh, right. Thank you."

Peter glanced through the classroom door and down the open hallway. Robin Sutter was halfway down the hall, weaving through the crowd of students. Peter stood alone, watching her, until the tardy bell jarred him from his thoughts.

Jake carried the card with him when the lunch bell rang. He stared at it, paying little attention to the other students in the corridor. His broad shoulders brushed against lockers and bumped against a support column, but he hardly noticed. He had to find Mattie Ramiro. The problem was that Mattie, at four feet eleven inches tall, was the world's most slippery kid. He tended to disappear among crowds, if you didn't know how to look for him.

Jake swept through a door into the cold outside air, passing a group of varsity football players. He hardly noticed. "There goes Mr. Sensitive," one of them murmured. "It's Clarinet Boy," another said, and a few guys laughed. Jake knew they didn't understand why a person his size was unwilling to tackle and crash into other players on a competitive team. But Jake wasn't bothered by what they said. Besides, he was on a mission.

He found Mattie in the student quad. He sat alone in the cold, shoulders hunched, his eyes focused on something, so intent he didn't even notice the pigeon pecking at the crust of his abandoned, half-eaten sandwich.

As Jake approached, his shadow fell across Mattie. "Hey," he said.

Mattie looked up. "Hey, it's Jake the Monster Man. Did you bring a granola bar? I'll trade you chips for it."

Jake nodded and exchanged with Mattie, who tucked the granola bar away.

"Whatcha working on?" Jake asked, sitting down next to him and absently removing his Superball from his pocket. He rolled it around in his hands. For some reason fidgeting with the tiny Superball helped him sort through his thoughts.

Mattie reached into his book bag and removed his Leatherman multi-tool. Once he selected the correct screwdriver from the several choices, he reached for the object Jake had seen him holding. It was an action figure, a twelve-inch reproduction of the world's most famous comic book super-hero: Hyperman. Mattie tugged at the hero's costume, pulling it away from the plastic to expose Hyperman's naked back. There, held in place by four screws, was a tiny door.

"Want to see how this works," Mattie mumbled, more to himself than to Jake.

The door came off quickly, and Mattie began probing the open hole with his screwdriver. He pried out a metallic device no bigger than a button, then held it up to the light. A disk lay in the center of it, and wires from this disk, exposed by Mattie's labors, trailed into Hyperman's chest.

"This is the battery," Mattie said, "and this is the sound chip." He touched his finger to a wire, and the wire made contact with a metal plate. An electrical connection resulted, and the device began to speak.

"I will fly to the rescue!" it said. Mattie grinned.

"Cool," said Jake.

Mattie touched the wire a second time.

"Surrender, villain!" said the chip.

"Before now," said Mattie, "they had to use tape or wire recorders to make a doll or an action figure talk. The units were really big, and they could usually only say one thing." Mattie reached for the screwdriver again and began reassembling the toy. "Today, though, they have sound chips. Chips are smaller, and you can put more information on them, so Hyperman here can say three or four different things."

Jake nodded. "It's amazing that you know all this stuff," he said. "And you're so fast. I mean, I can't believe how fast you can take something apart and put it back together."

Mattie shrugged. "Been doing it since I was about five years old, I guess." He slid the sound device back into Hyperman's hollow body.

Jake thought a moment. *Five years old? That was when Mattie's parents got divorced, when he started living with his grandparents.*

So, somehow around the time of the divorce, Mattie must have developed this knack, almost a compulsion, for taking things apart and putting them back together. He couldn't keep his hands off anything mechanical, that was for sure. It seemed that every time Jake ran into Mattie, pieces of a Walkman or a camcorder or some other electronic marvel lay scattered around the boy. Mattie would slip these pieces back together like a child assembling a simple wooden jigsaw puzzle. And he would do so with the coldest sort of concentration Jake had ever seen.

Jake realized that Mattie, as the son of divorced parents, had a hobby that grew not from the need to take things apart, but from the need to put them back together.

"Hey," said Jake, "how'd you manage this?" He held up the card. Mattie stopped his work and studied it a moment. "Not my doing," he said. "I got one too. Think they came from Peter?"

Jake shook his head. "Doubt it. He would have said something."

Mattie twirled in the last of the screws, then tugged Hyperman's uniform back into place. He stared at the toy, a strange, almost vacant expression on his face. "There," he said, "all together again."

Jake fumbled with his clarinet case, a little hesitant about leaving his friend. "Look," he said, "I'm going to skip lunch. I've got a piece I have to practice. We'll talk to Peter about the cards later, okay?"

Mattie looked up as if he were just noticing that Jake was there. "Huh? Oh, right. We'll see if Peter knows where they came from."

The four of them met in the courtyard after school.

Byte, Jake, and Mattie arrived from their sixth-period classes. Peter was already waiting for them. He was sitting on a stone bench, his jacket pulled around him and his back against a tree, his eyes glaring from behind a clump of fine, dark hair. He yanked his glasses off and set them on the bench beside him with an angry *clink*. His friends paused before coming too close.

"Peter, is this what I think it is?" asked Jake, drawing out the plastic card he'd received.

Mattie grinned and did a little celebratory skip-step. "It sure is. The semester ends tomorrow, and we have four-day guest passes to the comic book convention. It starts Thursday, ends Sunday, and I am *there!*"

"Aren't these expensive?" asked Jake.

"Thirty bucks apiece," said Mattie. "I checked."

Byte frowned. "Where did they come from?"

The group turned toward Mattie, but the youngest Misfit shook his head. "Now I'm insulted. I'm thrilled to have the badge, sure, but whoever delivered them had no style whatsoever. I mean, I found mine shoved in my lunch bag."

Peter rolled his eyes. "Where'd they *come* from?" he repeated. "Where else? They're from *her*. She knows Jake and Mattie are into comics, and she's using that somehow. She's up to something. I *know* her."

"Her?" Jake asked, shaking his head.

"You know, *her*," Mattie said.

Byte covered her mouth with her hand to keep from laughing out loud, and Peter glared at her.

"You know, this is a pretty nice gift, Peter," Byte said. "We should really send her a thank-you note or something." Then a positively evil gleam came to her eye. "You could maybe send *roses*...."

Peter raised his hands helplessly. "Can't you see what's happening here? She sneaked these to us without our knowing. She even used our secret emblem! Don't you know what this means?" His voice was taking on a shrill tone.

Byte, Jake, and Mattie just looked at one another. "I guess," Jake said, "it means we're going to a comic book convention. Are you coming with us?"

Peter looked up into the overcast sky, as though his logical world had just started rotating in the wrong direction. "I don't know. This has to be another one of Robin Sutter's competitive games."

Byte finally settled matters. "Well," she said, "here's what I think. I think you should go with us, Peter—and I think you should be grateful."

"Yeah!" said Mattie.

"That's right," said Jake.

Peter paused, then surrendered. "All right. Okay. I'll go.

Of course I'll go. Even though I think she's trying to buy her way into the Misfits, sneaking us *presents*. I'll try to be grateful," he grumbled. "Are you satisfied?"

"I'm satisfied," said Byte. She turned to Jake. "Are you satisfied?"

"I'm satisfied," said Jake.

The four of them started walking toward the campus parking lot.

"So," said Mattie, "are we going in costume? What panel discussions do you want to attend? Whose autographs do you want to get?" When no one answered his questions, he began tugging at Peter's sleeve. "Hey—hey! Isn't anyone going to ask me if *I'm* satisfied?"

chapter two

Thursday

As Peter walked up to the convention center, the first thing he saw was an alien with pink antennae, followed by a barbarian wearing a fake fur costume and swinging a plastic sword. As he gaped at these characters, a young boy running through the crowd smacked into him. "'Scuse me," the boy said, then he blasted Peter with a ray gun.

More strange creatures shuffled past—Klingons with rubber brow ridges, elves with green skin and latex pointed ears, fairy princesses wearing wings made of wire and Saran Wrap. It was, after all, a comic book convention, the Seventeenth Annual Bugle Point Comicon, and Peter was surrounded by a throng of enthusiastic comic book fans. Although some convention guests had arrived in costume, Peter was relieved to see that most of them had just worn everyday clothing. Peter himself was wearing plain old blue jeans and, under his jacket, a T-shirt celebrating his favorite comic book character, Hyperman.

"Peter! Hey, Peter!"

Peter turned in the direction of the voice. The crowd had thickened at the entrance, for the doors to the convention center had yet to open. Peter saw little more than a mass of eager faces. Then he noticed a bit of red flitting back and forth through the crowd, disappearing and reappearing, heading in his direction. Finally it came to a stop and stood next to Peter.

"Yo," Mattie said matter-of-factly.

Peter just stared at Mattie. *How does he do that?* he wondered.

"Let's go!" said Mattie. "What's holding things up?"

Peter shook his head. "Have you seen any of the others?"

"Hold my bag a minute," Mattie said. "But be careful. These are the comics I brought to be autographed." He climbed on top of a concrete trash receptacle to scan the crowd, then pointed to the middle of the swarm of people. "There."

In a moment, Peter saw Jake making his way through the crowd. While Mattie slipped through the cracks, Jake made his *own* cracks. He spotted Peter and Mattie, waved, and headed their way. People moved aside as he walked over to his friends. "Finally made it," he said.

"Hi," said a voice from behind him.

Peter smiled. Standing behind Jake, almost hidden, was Byte. She was wearing blue jeans, a baseball hat that said "Hyperman—the Movie" in gold letters, and an enormous Hyperman T-shirt that drooped from her shoulders and fell nearly to her knees.

"Okay, we're all here," said Peter dryly. "Let the revel begin."

The doors to the convention center opened, and the crowd surged through. Peter, Byte, Jake, and Mattie soon found themselves in an exhibit area that was serving as a sort of museum gallery. Comic book artists from across the nation were offering pencil sketches, pen-and-ink drawings, and even original watercolor paintings. Each piece was for sale at silent auction, the proceeds supporting the Comic Book Legal Defense Fund. Peter read the instructions:

> *Want to take it home? Each piece of artwork has a slip of paper hanging beside it. Write down your name, your convention badge number, and your bid. Winners will be announced at 4:00 P.M.*

His eyes moved quickly across the different works of art, and they fell upon a large oil painting of Hyperman. The hero looked gritty, tense, unshaven, the expression on his face taut and as clenched as his fists. Also, the colors of his uniform were darker and more metallic than they should have been: burgundy instead of red, violet instead of blue, deep golden bronze instead of yellow.

"Look at this," said Peter.

"Wow," exclaimed Jake. "Now that is awesome."

"Cool," said Mattie.

Byte looked doubtful. "Why does it look like he's wearing battle armor?" she asked. "I thought bullets bounced off this guy."

Jake and Mattie rolled their eyes and moved off to another display.

"Anyway," said Byte, looking at the portrait more closely, "I don't like it. I think he looks mean."

That's for sure, Peter thought. Peter had collected some very old Hyperman comics—a few went back to the 1940s—and he was used to a very different image of his favorite super-hero. The Hyperman Peter knew stood with a bright yellow cape flapping behind him in the wind, legs spread, fists at his hips, and grin on his face. The old Hyperman had a spark of fun; he would raise villains over his head, spin them around until they were dizzy, then drop them in a heap at police headquarters. But the '90s Hyperman of this painting looked as if he would just as soon rip the villains' heads off and be done with it. The image made Peter's heart sink.

"Come on," he said. "Let's look at something else."

They moved on, and a moment later Peter felt Jake's finger tapping on his shoulder. Considering Jake's size, even a light tapping was hard to ignore. Peter turned, and his friend motioned to a figure standing in the doorway.

"Our hostess," whispered Jake.

Robin Sutter spotted them and walked over. Peter tensed. There had always been something about Robin that set his alarms ringing. She hadn't spoken a word, but her folded arms, cocked head, and half-smile were warning enough.

But then, maybe he was just imagining things.

"Hi, everybody," said Robin. "Glad you could make it." She turned her smile on Peter. "So, Peter, have you checked your files yet?"

Peter nodded, eyeing her skeptically. Of course he had. At the end of every semester, Peter Braddock and Robin Sutter each went to the high school counseling office and requested to see an update of their cumulative files. Each semester their grade point averages were updated, and it was always a race to see which one had earned the higher score. Both Robin and Peter were at or near the top of their class, and each was terrified at the thought of coming in second to the other.

"So," said Robin, "let's have it. How did you do?"

Peter cleared his throat. "Well...." He hesitated, but then he realized there was no point in putting off the inevitable. One way or the other they would have to know each other's score. "I went up a little. 3.989."

Robin groaned. "I don't believe it," she said. "Mine went up too—3.987. But you're still *ahead* of me!"

Peter shook his head as though the difference didn't matter. It was a polite gesture, but it didn't much hide the fact that his day had just brightened considerably. "So," he said, "it's no big deal. Two hundredths of a grade point."

Robin's eyes narrowed. "Two *thousandths* of a grade point, Braddock. How do you keep your scores up with a math sense like that?" Then she smiled. "I'm gaining on you, though. You'd better be looking over your shoulder."

Like I'm not already? thought Peter.

"Hey, Robin," piped in Mattie, "you're wearing a volunteer badge, and you've got the Hyperman promo jacket and everything. How did you get to work at a neat place like this?"

Robin shrugged. "No big deal. My dad is an administrator here at the convention center. He asked me to help out. Besides," she said, and Peter noticed that her abrupt speaking manner softened, "our family kind of has a history in the comic book business."

Mattie, the biggest comic book fan in the group, suddenly perked up. "Hey—that's right!" he said. "Is your grandfather going to be here? Will he be signing autographs or doing any sketches?"

"Wait a minute," Jake said, suddenly realizing that the conversation had leaped ahead of him. "You mean you're related to *Joe* Sutter? The guy who invented Hyperman—what, sixty years ago?"

"That's right," said Robin. "Grandpa and his friend, Barry Nagel, created Hyperman when they were just teenagers. His friend wrote the stories, and Grandpa did all the artwork."

Peter's mind briefly flashed on the Hyperman painting he had just seen. He imagined what it would have looked like if Hyperman's creator had painted it. His voice dropped almost to a whisper. "Wow," he said. "I'd love to have a Hyperman sketch by Joe Sutter himself. What a collector's piece that would be."

Robin heard him, and her face took on a saddened look. "Sorry," she said. "Grandpa won't be here. I asked him to come, but he said no conventions. He said he didn't want to talk about Hyperman, didn't want to look at Hyperman, didn't want to think about Hyperman."

Peter and his friends glanced at one another. *What's that all about?* Peter thought. *An artist who hates his creation?* Peter had grown up on Hyperman. His *father* had grown up on Hyperman. Hyperman, in six decades, had become a cultural icon. There was something very sad about what Robin was saying. It was almost like hearing about a parent hating a child.

No one spoke for a long, awkward moment, and Robin's cheeks reddened with embarrassment. Byte, Jake, and Mattie didn't know what to say, because none of them really knew Robin all that well. And though Peter had been in various classes with her since the sixth grade, his relationship with Robin had always been one of competition rather than friendship.

Why, then, did she invite us here? Peter wondered.

"Anyway," Robin said, changing the subject, "if I can help you find anything, let me know." Her face brightened. "What did you want to see first?"

Mattie reached into his rear pocket and took out a folded booklet. It was the convention guide, a moment-by-moment calendar of all the events the convention was offering over the next four days. "Hey, they're showing a preview of the new Hyperman movie in just a few minutes," he said. "I don't want to miss that."

"Right," said Robin. "That's in the lecture hall. I'd walk you over there, but unfortunately I have to help my dad. You know how it is." She smiled. Her fingers absently played with her class ring, twirling it back and forth on her finger. "The hall is upstairs, first set of double doors on the left. I'll try to meet you later. Enjoy the show."

She headed off into the crowd.

Peter leaned forward to watch Robin disappear into the crowd, and Byte nudged him in the ribs with her elbow.

"You know, Peter," she said, smiling, "Robin's kind of cute. I think she likes you."

Peter stared at Byte as though she had grown two heads. He had known Byte fairly well since the beginning of high school, and he still hadn't found the nerve tell her he liked *her*. Now he was supposed to think of Robin Sutter...as a *girlfriend?* The idea was preposterous. It was absurd. Then his mind flashed to the brutal lesson in logic Robin had provided to their debate opponents. Well, maybe the idea was a *little* interesting, but Peter certainly wasn't going to pursue it. And anyway, why did it have to be Byte's idea?

"No, really," said Byte. "I'm serious."

"Let's stay within the realm of planet Earth, all right?" said Peter. *Robin Sutter and me? It would never work.* "Besides," he said, "even if she is cute—and I'm not

34 saying she is—we'd still never get along. She's so…so…*arrogant*."

He looked at his friends for support, but all three of them were frozen, staring at him. They began to chuckle.

"What?" said Peter.

His uncomprehending look caused more peals of laughter. Mattie's eyes watered, and Jake's broad shoulders shook as he laughed. Finally Byte, catching her breath, hooked her arm at Peter's elbow and patted his hand.

"It's all right, Peter," she said. "We love you even if you are clueless."

"What?" said Peter. "What?…"

The lecture hall was a small auditorium with a sloping floor, carpeted walls to absorb sound, and the kind of springy chairs found in movie theaters. It seated, according to Peter's estimate, about five hundred people, and judging by the crowd he'd seen outside the center, today it would be packed. Byte followed behind him as he walked down the jammed center aisle, looking for four empty seats. Jake, picking up the rear, took advantage of his height to scout the room.

"I think we're stuck with sitting in the back," he said.

The only one missing was Mattie. Mattie had moved ahead of them, slipping through the crowd like a phantom.

"Wait a minute," said Jake, then he smiled and pointed. "There!"

35

Just a few rows from the front, directly in the center—
in perhaps the best seat in the room—was Mattie. He
stood waving his thin arms to them like an airline
flagger guiding in a 747. Next to him were three empty
seats. He smiled proudly and gave a thumbs-up as the
other Misfits worked their way over to him. His jacket
guarded one seat, his convention guide the next, and his
History of the AC Universe the third.

"What took you so long?" he asked when they arrived.

"Nice going," Jake exclaimed, quickly settling his large
frame into the seat.

Mattie grinned. "It's my job. I'm God's gift to the
terminally slow."

Most of the crowd had found seats as well, though
several dozen stragglers were still milling about in the
aisles. Many, too late for seats, leaned against the walls or
stood in the back.

Peter's eyes, darting here and there, fell on several of
these stragglers. A heavyset, bearded man munched
popcorn from an immense cardboard tub. A set of identical male twins each wore a T-shirt sporting half of
Hyperman's face, so that when they stood together they
formed one complete portrait. A child, perhaps four
years old, sat sleepily on his father's shoulders, his cheek
resting on his father's head.

As he looked over the crowd, Peter thought of his
father, Nick Braddock, special agent for the FBI. Peter
had learned a lot about the skills of observation and
deduction from his dad. He and his father often played

36 a game: What could Peter guess about his father's day just by observing his father closely at the day's end? Peter had become a master at The Game, practicing it every chance he got. If Peter spied a spot of black at his father's shirt sleeve, he knew that Nick Braddock had done a great deal of paperwork that day (Peter's father had a habit of resting his arm on the stack of papers on his desk, and he often picked up stray smudges of ink). If Peter noticed a light sheen of sweat on his father's skin, he knew that Nick had supervised some training at the FBI obstacle course that afternoon. More often than not, by the time Peter gave his father a good looking-over, he knew where Nick Braddock had gone that day, what he had done, even what he had ordered for lunch.

Peter let his eyes wander over the crowd. Most of the people in the lecture hall were talking with friends, laughing, or just waiting for the event to begin. A few, however, piqued Peter's curiosity. One man sat with his shoulders hunched and his arms tightly folded. He glowered fiercely at the empty seat in front of him. Then a young woman in a brown, hooded robe caught Peter's eye. Her face was shadowed by the hood, and she walked up and down the aisles passing out what looked like shiny, gold foil coins.

But Peter's eyes locked on one fidgeting straggler in par-ticular. The young man's eyes darted about anxiously—first at the stage, then at the projection screen, then at the large 70mm movie projector in the back of the room.

Start with observations, thought Peter. The man was large, Peter saw, and tremendously overweight. He wore a black T-shirt that had long ago faded to gray—the yellowed remains of a picture of Deathwatch, a popular Mercenary Comics villain, still faintly visible across his chest. His long black hair was pulled back into a straggly ponytail. Peter estimated the young man to be in his late twenties.

Byte whispered, "It's not polite to stare."

"Yeah," Peter whispered back, "but look at that guy. Look at the way he's acting. There's something odd about him. Look at his eyes."

The man's lips moved as though he were speaking, but there was no one standing next to him. He was talking to himself, muttering like a child with an imaginary playmate. His left hand jerked at his side, tapping uncontrollably against his leg.

He's very nervous, thought Peter. *He's not just waiting for the movie to start. There's something else. The way he's looking around, he's really checking things out.* Peter had no way of knowing if the man was just odd, or if he was really up to something devious.

At that moment, the young man, in one of his nervous glances around the room, noticed that Peter was staring at him. As their eyes locked, the man seemed to study Peter's face, and his lips ceased their silent mumbling. He shrank back against the wall, continuing to eye Peter.

Peter felt a nudge. "You done playing detective, Sherlock?" asked Jake.

The interruption slammed a door on Peter's thoughts. "Huh?"

"Show's about to start."

Peter wasn't quite ready to let go. "Jake," he said, "take a good look at that guy over there in the black T-shirt leaning against the wall, the one looking at us. What do you think?"

Jake glanced past Peter and studied the young man. "Search me," he said. "There're a lot of strange-looking people here." He gestured toward an elderly, heavyset man wearing a homemade, skintight super-hero outfit. The man clutched an aluminum briefcase to his body as though the case contained state secrets. "For example, that bizarre gentleman over there."

A man leaped to the stage and stood at the podium, smiling a huge artificial smile. The audience, grateful that something was finally happening, greeted him with a burst of applause.

The man's smile cracked even wider, and he motioned to the crowd for silence. "Welcome," he said, "and thank you for coming."

Peter turned to get one more look at the stranger in the T-shirt, but the young man had vanished.

"Hey—" said Peter.

Byte touched his shoulder. "Shhh!"

"As you know," the man at the podium was saying, "next year will mark the sixtieth anniversary of the world's most popular adventure character, Hyperman. In the 1940s, Hyperman was the star of two popular movie serials. In the 1950s, the Hyperman TV series ran for seven seasons, and has since been viewed in over a hundred countries and translated into dozens of languages.

"The Bugle Point Comicon organizers are proud to dedicate this year's convention to the world's first—and greatest—super-hero. We are even prouder to bring to you today's presentation. *Hyperman: The Movie* will premiere June 14 in over 2600 theaters nationwide. Hunter Brothers Studios and American Comics are thrilled to give you, Hyperman's biggest fans, a sneak preview. The film is, even as we speak, undergoing some finishing touches, but you will essentially see the entire movie from beginning to end."

The audience exploded in cheers and whistles. Everywhere around him, Peter saw people clapping madly. The excitement was contagious. In spite of his carefully cultivated reserve, Peter found himself clapping as loudly as everyone else.

"Finally," Byte said, "you're starting to loosen up a little."

The lights began to dim, and Peter settled into the expectations of the moment—darkness, a period of silence and anticipation, a hum as the projector started, then the flickering of light against the screen as the sneak preview began.

But instead of the hum of a movie projector, an explosion shattered the silence, followed by a keening whistle like that of a bottle rocket. Peter saw a spurt of red flame, and a burst of sparks bloomed above the stage. Another explosion sent up a blue plume that burned like a

40 Roman candle. The whistle of one firework overlapped the next. They sounded, Peter thought, like children screaming. There came another flash, and great, flowering sparks of yellow and blue joined the fading cloud of red. Many fans covered their heads; others tried to crouch beneath their seats. A handful made it to the exits. A girl near Peter screeched and batted her hands at her hair where some sparks had landed.

"Keep down!" someone near them shouted. "And cover your heads!"

Fireworks continued to explode and light up the room, but now a strange smell tainted the air as well. The auditorium began to fill with pink smoke. It started at floor level and swelled in great, swirling gusts where people moved through it. More explosions followed, pounding in Peter's chest and vibrating through the carpeted floor. Peter's ears began to ring. Soon his throat burned, and his eyes began to water, but even so he noticed the rustling in the air above him. He looked up at the narrow metal catwalk circling the room near the ceiling—designed, Peter supposed, to help workers mount light fixtures or repair the air conditioning.

Peter gasped. Right now someone was up there, running along the catwalk. Smoke obscured his view, but he was certain he saw a hooded figure dressed in purple boots and tights, a long cape billowing behind him. The hooded figure carried large, metallic discs in his arms, canisters of some kind. The red mouth painted on his mask was opened wide, as though he were laughing insanely.

"Look!" shouted Peter, grabbing Byte's arm.

The hooded figure was close to the darkened stage. Near him was a metal ladder, and above him a small trap door that no doubt led to the roof. For a moment, just as its gloved hand reached for the ladder, the figure fell into a shaft of light and Peter saw it clearly for the first time.

It can't be. It isn't possible....

But it was. It was *him*. The Jester. It seemed as if Hyperman's greatest enemy had come alive and stepped out of the pages of a comic book. Peter gazed up at him, and the Jester paused and turned. The masked face looked down in Peter's direction. Could the Jester possibly know that Peter was looking at him? Then their eyes met, and Peter felt a chill, because he sensed—he *knew*—that beneath the mask the Jester was grinning at him. In between the explosions of fireworks, Peter could make out the eerie, echoing laugh of the Jester. The Jester bowed, as though accepting applause for his little show. Then, in one easy motion, he swung himself onto the ladder and opened the trap door. Sunlight burst into the room, and the villain was gone.

Mattie, too, had seen movement on the catwalk. He gazed upward in time to see the Jester and, like Peter, he noted the way the villain clung to large silver disks as he ran.

But as Mattie watched, a Roman candle burst nearby, its wail a stinging shriek in Mattie's left ear. He clamped his hands over his ears and huddled half-under his seat for protection. Above him, the Roman candle sent up a fountain of red and gold sparks, which rained down on Mattie's head and the back of his neck.

He looked up. People were rushing toward the exits. Peter grabbed Byte's arm and pointed toward the catwalk, but Mattie was too close to the ground to see what Peter was seeing. Instead Mattie peered through the crack between the seats ahead of him. Through it he could just make out the film screen, and he stared at what appeared there. A huge square of light played across the screen, and inside the square, red letters spelled out a strange poem. After a few moments, the image on the screen began to blacken. The poem grew darker, becoming a circle of black that expanded until the entire message peeled away and melted.

Mattie remembered the metal canisters and the huge movie projector in the back of the room. He could think of only one explanation: Those canisters—the ones the Jester had clutched to his body as he escaped—contained reels of film.

The Jester had stolen the Hyperman movie.

chapter three

having witnessed the Jester's theft, and eager to help if they could, the Misfits went looking for Robin Sutter. They found her in her father's office.

Jonathon Sutter paced the room as he spoke into a cordless telephone. Robin followed behind him, seeming to have no purpose or goal other than staying close to her father. A uniformed police officer—called in from the street, where he had been directing convention traffic—stood near the door, silent. The officer was tall and barrel-chested, and he held a palm-sized spiral notebook, which he flipped open, waiting for Sutter to finish his call.

"I've already called the insurance company," Sutter was saying, his words clipped and angry. "Yes, we're covered, but that's not my problem now. I want more security around here—our in-house staff is not big enough. And I mean real security—uniforms, weapons, the whole bit. I don't *care* how much it costs."

44   He slammed the phone down onto its cradle, leaned against his desk, and rubbed his eyes. His fingers then moved to his temples and slowly massaged them.

Robin put her hand on her father's arm. "Is it really that bad?" she asked.

Jonathon Sutter gave Robin's hand a little squeeze. "Don't worry, honey," he said. "We'll get through it."

Peter cleared his throat, and both Robin and her father turned their heads in his direction. Neither had been aware that the Misfits were in the office.

"Oh, Daddy," said Robin. Her face was flushed, and she looked as though she might be on the verge of crying. "These are the friends I was telling you about—Peter, Byte, Jake, and Mattie."

Mr. Sutter nodded a greeting and went to sit at his desk.

"We thought the police might want us to make a statement," offered Peter. "Actually, it was hard to see anything. The Jester set up a pretty impressive distraction."

"So I heard," said Mr. Sutter.

Robin watched her father. *The lines around her eyes,* Peter thought, *belong to someone much older than sixteen.* Funny—as much as he wanted to dislike Robin, as much as his competitive spirit wanted to be *brainier* than she was, he did not enjoy seeing her this unhappy.

"Okay," said Robin, "so let's look at the bright side." She seemed to force herself to stand a little straighter. "The loss is covered by insurance, right? So the convention center isn't out any money, except for maybe the deductible. And second, it's not as though the stolen movie print was the *only* one in existence, right? The studio probably has a dozen more, at least. So really, what's the big deal here?"

Her father picked up a pencil and tapped it thoughtfully against his desktop. "I'm afraid, honey," he said, "that it's not that simple. It's more than a matter of reimbursing Hunter Brothers Studios for the cost of a few reels of film."

Mattie nodded. "Video piracy."

The police officer snorted.

"Exactly," said Mr. Sutter. "Whoever stole the movie now has a master print. He can, with the right equipment, make copies onto videotape and sell them. The release of the movie is months away. Imagine how many copies of a bootleg video this Jester could sell in that time." Mr. Sutter took a deep breath. "In two weeks, every unscrupulous comic book shop in the country will be selling pirated copies of *Hyperman: The Movie*. There will be ads in underground magazines— ads we won't even know about, let alone be able to trace. The studio will lose ticket sales, and if we can't stop it from happening, the convention center will lose a fortune in future revenues. Who's going to want to hold a convention here if we can't guarantee basic security?"

Robin twirled a lock of hair around her finger, wrapping it, tugging it absently, angrily. "I didn't realize it was this serious."

46

"It is," he said, "but I'll take care of it."

"Mr. Sutter," said Byte, "video manufacturers sometimes put Macrovision on their videos for copy protection. Is there something like that for film? I mean, is there any chance the thief won't be able to *make* a usable copy of the Hyperman movie?"

Mattie meekly raised his hand. "I saw something," he said.

"I just don't know, Byte," said Mr. Sutter, "but it's a good thought. I'll look into it."

"The thief wore a pretty accurate and sophisticated costume," added Peter. "Someone might want to check local costume shops for rentals."

"I saw something," Mattie repeated.

Mr. Sutter picked up the telephone and punched in another number. As it rang, he looked at Robin and the Misfits. "Why don't you and your friends go grab some lunch," he said. "I've got a lot to do here."

Mattie stared at the food on the table in front of him. "While we're talking about crooks," he said, "we should start with the guy who decided that five-fifty was a fair price for a hot dog and a Coke."

Jake Armstrong studied the last three inches of his hot dog, crumpled it into his mouth, chewed once, then swallowed. "So, Peter," he said, using his finger to swipe a drop of mustard from his chin, "what's next?"

Peter shook his head. "I'm not sure."

Peter was distracted, confused by images of the convention, of the Jester looking right at him, and of Robin Sutter.

Robin had taken only a bite of her food, and was staring at her drink as she slowly swirled it with a straw. "I didn't realize that my dad was going to be so upset about this," she said. "He doesn't usually get so worried. I guess this is bigger than I thought."

Peter's thoughts went back to the theft of the film. "You know," he said, "this Jester character certainly planned well. It couldn't have been easy to set up all those fireworks—"

"Not to mention the smoke bombs," Mattie said, reaching for the crust of Byte's microwaved pizza. Byte slapped his fingers. "Ow! Anyway, my eyes are still sore."

"So," Peter continued, "who would have the motivation to steal the film and would actually do it?"

"Anyone interested in a lot of quick money," Jake replied. "Meaning anyone."

"But we should explore the possibilities—" Peter began.

"Braddock," Robin said, pressing her napkin to her lips, then wadding it up and flinging it on the table. "I hate to break it to you, but the Jester's already gotten away with the film. The guy's not *stupid*, okay? We can't trace him, and he's not going to hold onto the film forever. So give it up. Let the police handle it."

Mattie reached for a clean napkin and began scribbling something on it. "I don't think so," he said.

Everyone turned to look at him.

"We do have a lead to follow." He continued writing for another moment, then turned the napkin around so the others could see it. "The Jester will be back," Mattie said. "While he was stealing the Hyperman movie, he placed a film slide on the projector. The slide had this message on it. The Jester accidentally—or maybe on purpose—put the slide too close to the projection lamp, so it melted after a few seconds. With all the fireworks and confusion, I'd be surprised if anyone else even noticed it."

Peter and the others stared at the clue.

> *On Saturn's eve, in darkness' smoke,*
> *A tale to tell, a whisper spoke,*
> *An old man's trial, the Jester's smile,*
> *Now turn upon a hero's cloak.*

"In the comics, the Jester's clues are never about the crime he just committed," Mattie continued. "They're about his *next* crime. I'm telling you, he's coming back."

"Now that's a fun thought," Byte remarked.

Mattie nodded. "And there's something else."

He reached for the stack of comic books he had brought with him to the convention. Grabbing a fistful, he began rifling through them. When he finally found the one he was looking for, he held it up, studied it for a moment, then slapped it down on the table.

"There!" he cried, and his voice carried more than a hint of triumph.

The others stared at him blankly.

"Wow, Mattie," Jake teased. "It's a comic book, and it's got your fingerprints all over it. Okay, you have the right to remain silent—"

"*No*," said Mattie. "Look at the cover."

They all stared down at the comic book. It was last summer's *Hyperman Annual*. The cover featured a grinning Jester, cackling madly as he held a chunk of glowing, radioactive mycronite over a "dying" Hyperman. The Jester was wearing a familiar costume: purple suit with yellow pinstripes, domino mask, and purple top hat.

"Look," Mattie said, "how long has the Jester been wearing this costume?"

"Oh, only about thirty years," said Jake. "What's your point?"

Mattie tapped his index finger on the cover of the comic. "Okay," he said, "but is this the costume the Jester was wearing *today*?"

"Well—no," said Byte. "He was wearing a different costume. The suit was the same color, but he had a purple cape with a hood instead of the top hat. And his mask covered his whole face, not just the area around his eyes."

"Right," said Mattie. "The Jester we saw today was wearing the old costume, the original one from the 1940s."

"Man, I can't believe I overlooked that," said Jake. "So what do you think it means?"

"For what it's worth," said Mattie, "I think it means that our Jester is not just some crazed fanboy out to grab the ultimate collectible. Whoever wore that costume knows the history. He's *into* comics—the expensive ones from the Golden Age."

Robin shook her head. "Not necessarily," she told him. "A lot of 1940s Hyperman appearances have been reprinted a dozen times—in the annuals, or as back stories in the one-hundred-page comics from the seventies. For that matter, the entire first year's run is available in the hardcover MasterSeries editions, and they're less than five years old. The thief doesn't have to be into Golden Age collecting. With all the material available, he could have gotten into the hobby yesterday."

"Still—" said Peter, doubtful.

Robin threw up her hands. "Fine," she said. "Who am I to be the cloud over your picnic? If you want, I suppose we can go back to my dad's office and share your theory with him."

Peter thought a moment. "We don't know enough yet," he said. "Actually, I was thinking we might learn more if we went straight to the source and talked to your grandfather."

"That's a *great* idea!" cried Mattie. "Joe Sutter can tell us anything we might need to know about Hyperman *or* the Jester."

"Right," said Jake. "He'd know more about the history of the Jester than anybody! Who knows, maybe the

Jester's riddle came from some old comic story that we don't even know about."

Robin slurped the last drops of soda from her cup, saying nothing, drawing out the moment. She stabbed into the ice with her straw as she pondered Jake's suggestion. "I don't know," she said. "You just don't understand what's going on with my grandfather."

"You want to tell us about it?" asked Peter.

Robin tossed the cup into a trash can. "No," she said. "There wouldn't be any point." She looked at the others. "Well, come on," she said. "Let's go."

Byte stood, tossed away the remnants of her lunch, and picked up the nylon bag containing her computer. Its weight felt natural as it hung from her shoulder by a strap—so natural, in fact, that being without it gave her a slight sense of unbalance, as though she were wearing only one shoe.

She was following her friends toward the exit doors when someone touched her shoulder. It was Robin. She had lagged behind the group and come up to Byte from behind. "Byte, listen," she said, "can I ask you something?"

"Sure."

"Okay," said Robin, "here goes. You know how there's a dance, a costume party, and all the other convention stuff going on this weekend?"

Byte nodded.

"Well, Dad decided it would be more convenient for us to stay at the hotel across the street rather than commute in every day from home."

"Uh, that's nice."

"So you see," said Robin, "I'm stuck inside this hotel room by myself all night. There's cable, and some money if I want to send out for pizza, but there's no one to talk to." Robin clawed her fingers through her hair and ruffled it out. "Can you imagine? Me, with no one to talk to? It's like Chinese water torture. So I'm asking if maybe you can stay there with me tomorrow. It'll be, I don't know, like a sleepover or something."

"Like a slumber party," offered Byte.

Robin nodded, then shrugged as though Byte were only half correct. "Right—well, that is, if you and I constitute a *party*."

Byte laughed, but the laughter came mostly from nervousness. For as long as she cared to remember, her only real friends had been Peter, Jake, Mattie, and—more importantly—the machine she was carrying. Staring at a monitor was so much less *risky* than staring into a human face.

"So," said Robin, "do I need to submit this proposal in writing or something?"

"Noooo," said Byte, laughing a little more easily.

"Do you need to call your mom and ask her if it's okay?"

Byte gripped her computer bag and thought about the phone in the convention center office. She could use it to send a message to her mom. "Not exactly," she said to Robin. "We don't work that way. If I e-mail her now, I can lay out in writing all the reasons why she should say yes, and she'll have plenty of time to think about it before she gets home from work. That way, I'm less likely to get a 'no' just because she's tired and grumpy."

"Have you ever thought about taking debate?" asked Robin. "You'd be really good."

Charles Leach, assistant editor at Mercenary Comics, sat at a booth on the main convention floor. In the dealer room, the heart of any comic book convention, everyone who had anything to do with the comic book profession—the artists, the writers, the publishers, the distributors, even the individual comic shop owners—gathered together in one warehouse-sized area. The ultimate goal at each booth, second only to having fun, was the organized and happy exchange of comic books for dollars.

But Charles Leach was having no fun at all.

A long line of comic fans stood at the Mercenary booth, drawn by the current marketing campaign. The Razorclaw one-shot, with its dramatic "Heads—You Lose!" cover illustration, had a release date timed to coincide with the convention, and Mercenary had arranged for the book's creative team to appear and sign copies. They were doing so now. Charles sat at the other end of the table, his arm moving in lazy boredom as he passed out "Mercenary Rules!" buttons and Razorclaw promo posters to the fans who didn't actually want to buy the comic.

A shadow fell over his table. "Pick up lunch for you, Mr. Leach?" said a voice.

Charles could not help but make a quick comparison between himself and the young man standing before him. Charles was trim, scrubbed, and frequently wore suits to the office, a place where most of the other employees worked in blue jeans. In contrast, Wilson Dominic wore a pair of dirty trousers and an ancient black T-shirt. The shirt didn't quite reach his waist, and his belly rolled out from beneath it. Dominic was nervously tapping his thumb against his hip the way a bass guitar player might slap at a string. Gazing up at him, Charles flipped over a small ad slick, stole a glance at his fellow workers to make sure they were occupied, and pretended to write down a lunch order.

Were we successful?

Dominic read the upside-down words and nodded.

Good, Charles wrote. *Make preparations for tomorrow's handoff. Contact me only if urgent.* Dominic was a Neanderthal, Charles told himself. There was no sense in spending any more time around him than necessary.

Wilson Dominic read the instructions and nodded one last time. He folded the ad slick and turned to leave, but then paused. He turned back to face Charles, then, blinking, he stared up at the fluorescent lights on the ceiling.

"Is there something else?" asked Charles, sighing.

Dominic sneaked a look past Charles's shoulder. It was clear he did not want any of the other Mercenary Comics employees to hear what he was about to say. He moved a little closer to Charles, forcing the editor to lean back and hold his breath.

"When I was in the lecture hall," Dominic whispered, "some high school kids were staring at me."

At those words, Charles threw a quick look to his right and noticed that the current editor of the *X-Mutant* titles was looking in his direction. He clamped his mouth shut and tried not to scream at the idiot standing before him. He gestured to Dominic for the ad slick and scribbled large letters full of sharp angles, pressing so hard he tore a gash in the paper. *If someone connects you with this....*

Dominic blinked again and said nothing. Charles glared at him, shook his head, and once more began writing.

Did they see you leave? Is it possible they saw anything important?

Dominic thought a moment, then shook his head.

Then the plan might not be compromised after all, Charles assured himself. He scribbled again on the ad slick. *Probably nothing to concern ourselves about,* he wrote. *But from now on, be more cautious! I won't tolerate carelessness.*

Charles slid the paper across the table and watched as Dominic wandered off to a distant trash can, tore the note into tiny bits, and dropped them inside.

Charles wondered at the wisdom of including Dominic in this venture. Clearly it would have been wiser to handle every detail of the plan himself, but as it happened, Charles did not have that option. Dominic had one skill, and Charles needed that skill to fulfill his plans. Dominic's participation was not only helpful, it was vital.

Charles only hoped the fool's blundering wouldn't be the ruin of them both.

Joe Sutter lived in a two-bedroom house surrounded by a tiny, unkempt lawn. Grass grew through cracks in the concrete walkway, and some bricks had fallen from the front steps.

Mattie had assumed that Joe Sutter, after collecting Hyperman royalties for almost sixty years, was a wealthy man. Now he realized that was not the case. Saddened by what he saw, he found himself walking more hesitantly toward the house.

"Come on in, guys," said Robin. "I'll get him. In the meantime, don't make too much noise, in case he's sleeping. And don't ask him too many questions. I really don't think he can help us much, and it just—well, it just opens up some old wounds."

She swung open the screen door, and the Misfits walked in behind her.

The inside of the house was as shabby as the outside. A worn wooden floor, a fraying rug, and a faded,

Tiffany-style lamp greeted the visitors as they stepped into the living room. Through an open doorway they could see an aging sofa and the only apparent concession to the 1990s—a forty-two inch, wide-screen color television set.

Mattie gazed at the two rooms. While the others chattered about the convention, the Jester, and the stolen film, he remained silent. Joe Sutter was a hero to Mattie, and he just wanted a few moments alone to absorb the idea that he was standing in Joe Sutter's home.

A splash of color above the fireplace caught his attention, and he saw something so beautiful, so filled with color and motion and life, he could not have spoken even if he wanted to.

From behind him he heard Jake gasp. "Oh, *wow.*"

Above the fireplace was an original oil painting of Hyperman. The hero stood against a red background. His legs were spread, his chest flexed, and a huge grin brightened his face. His arm muscles snapped the chains binding him, and bullets careened off his chest. The artist—no doubt Joe Sutter himself—had even added a dialogue balloon that was pure 1940s super-hero camp. "Take it easy, boys," Hyperman was saying. "Those bullets tickle!"

"That's amazing," Peter said quietly.

A squeaking sound came from the entryway. The group turned as Robin followed an elderly man in a wheelchair into the room. He was dressed in pajamas and a robe. His hair was white and looked unwashed,

58 and a week's growth of gray stubble dotted his neck and chin. He looked ancient—puffy nose, wrinkles, sagging cheeks, and thick glasses that made his eyes look large. Sutter's fingers were gnarled and misshapen.

Robin bent to kiss him on the cheek. "Grandpa," she said, "I brought some friends by to meet you."

Joe Sutter stared at the group without speaking, and the silence in the room grew painful. The man's body was small and almost curled up, trapped in the wheelchair, but his eyes were fiercely alive.

"Grandpa," said Robin, "these are my friends—Peter, Byte, Jake, and Mattie."

Sutter nodded.

"It's a pleasure to meet you, sir," said Mattie.

"That's for sure," added Jake.

A long, silent moment passed.

"We've been admiring your painting," Peter said. "It's breathtaking. We're all big fans of your work, and we'd love to see more of it. Why don't you do gallery showings or conventions?"

Mattie and the others looked at Peter, a little shocked at his boldness.

"Peter," said Robin, "that's not very—"

"Young man," said Sutter, leaning forward in his chair, trembling as he spoke. "Conventions just fill the wallets of those monsters at American Comics, and I'll have nothing to do with it." His fist pounded once, weakly, against the arm of his wheelchair.

"Why?" Mattie asked, puzzled. "Why do you hate American Comics?"

Sutter, gazing up at the painting on the wall, said nothing. Robin placed her hand on her grandfather's shoulder.

"Grandpa," she said, "has had…some problems… dealing with AC in the past. He's not on the best of terms with them."

"Let's not get into that," Sutter growled.

"Well, Grandpa," said Robin loudly, "you have to talk about it sometime. You're ticked off at them, and you have a right to be."

Sutter remained silent for a long while, his knuckles stretched white as he squeezed the armrests of his wheelchair. "They—they stole him from me," he finally said.

"Sir?" asked Peter.

"Back in 1938," Sutter explained, "when my friend Barry Nagel and I created Hyperman, no one knew how popular he would turn out to be. The people at American Comics—they were American Periodical Publications back then—weren't sure they wanted to take a chance on him. Oh, they would publish Hyperman, but only if Barry Nagel and Joe Sutter signed over all the rights. We did. For one hundred and twenty-nine dollars."

Sutter shook his head, reliving that moment in 1938. "You see," he said, "no one knew. Sixty years? Who would have guessed Hyperman would last that long? Who would have guessed he'd last six months? For two kids

60 just out of high school, right after the Depression, a hundred and twenty-nine dollars was a fortune."

"But surely there was more money than that," said Peter. "All the comic books you drew—"

"Oh, yes," said Sutter. "Barry got paid for every story he wrote. I got paid for every page I drew. But we were...employees. There were no royalties. We had no ownership or control over what they did with the character we had dreamed up. So when AC licensed the Hyperman products—the lunch boxes, the action figures, the towels, the peanut butter, the skateboards, the kites, the coin banks, and all kinds of toys—my character brought in millions of dollars in merchandising. The company made a fortune, and they kept every single penny."

"You got *nothing?*" asked Jake.

Sutter nodded. "That was the contract we signed," he said.

"That's not fair!" Mattie shouted. "You were so young! You didn't know what you were signing away. Mr. Sutter, you should do something. Take them to court—"

Sutter laughed dryly. "Court? Do you know how many times I've been in a courtroom? I've tried one lawsuit after another."

Robin sighed. "It's been tough," she said. "It seems the law protects you from being cheated, but it doesn't protect you from being young and naive. They say Grandpa signed away his rights fair and square."

Joe Sutter sat hunched over in his chair as though years of anger had twisted his body into something dry and cold and empty.

"In the late seventies," continued Robin, "there was a letter-writing campaign among comic book fans. The press got wind of it, and the bad publicity made American Comics a little uncomfortable. They agreed to pay Grandpa and Mr. Nagel's widow a small annual stipend. That's what Grandpa's been living on."

Mattie shook his head. "You could do interviews," he suggested eagerly, "talk at conventions. American would have to renegotiate the contract. They would—"

Sutter silenced him with a look. "I can't," he said. "No, son, they've covered everything. The contract I signed to receive the stipend forbids me from speaking out in public against American Comics. If I do, I lose the stipend. And I won't make myself a hypocrite by going to conventions, promoting the character, or drawing sketches just to add to a corporation's bottom line. American Comics may own Hyperman, son, but they don't own *me*." He pointed to the painting above the fireplace. "That may be all I have left," he said, "but I imagined it. I painted it. It's *mine*. And they can't take it away from me."

"But you're Hyperman's *creator*," insisted Mattie. "He *belongs* to you."

Joe Sutter stiffened. "I'm not the creator of the Hyperman you see in today's comics. I can't bear what they've done with him. They've made him…*hostile,* and cynical. They said they were going to 'update' him, and all they've done is turn him into a clone of all the other cheap, overmuscled thugs they call heroes today. I'm surprised they don't have him carrying a gun." His words grew louder and more forceful. "It turns my stomach, what they've done to my…my brainchild. Now, you want me to go to their shows, help them market their 'product'?" Sutter grimaced. "I'll see the whole lot of them in hell first."

"Grandpa!" Robin said.

"Okay," Mattie persisted, "forget about them. Think of yourself. You could do sketches and paintings. You wouldn't have to wear an 'I love American Comics' button. A lot of comic book artists from the forties and fifties make a good living that way—Bob Kane did for years. And they get the recognition they deserve."

Sutter shook his head. "Thank you, son," he said, "for trying so hard. But look at me. Look at my arthritic hands." He held up his gnarled and twisted fingers.

"Paint a picture?" said Joe Sutter. "Heck, son, I can barely hold a spoon."

When the visit ended, Robin and the Misfits headed toward Peter's car, a cherry red, 1969 Volkswagen Beetle convertible. Mattie, not uttering a sound, climbed in the back and yanked viciously at the seat belt.

Peter turned to Robin. "You were right," he said quietly. "We didn't learn much, and we just made your grandfather feel worse. I wanted to ask more questions…but it just didn't seem worth it."

"It's not your fault," she replied. "You were only trying to help."

"I really am sorry about your grandfather," Peter said. "He's been through a lot—and on top of it all, he's confined to that wheelchair. May I ask what caused that?"

Robin just shook her head. "I don't think there's anything wrong with Grandpa's legs. I'm sure he could walk again if he tried—he just chooses not to. Like he chooses not to paint."

"But why?"

Robin stared back at the house. "I don't know," she said, her voice distant. "He just says he's tired. I think he's given up."

chapter
four

Friday

the sun was shining, a cool wind was blowing, and the morning seemed to hold more promise of fun than of masked criminals, daring thefts, or thrilling escapes. This was, after all, day two of the comic book convention. There was a lot to see, enough to distract even the most determined group of teen detectives.

Jake and Mattie strolled near the publishers' area. American Comics had spent thousands to create a booth that would grab a fan's attention. A seven-foot-tall mechanical alien guarded the entire display. The alien held a ray-gun, and it turned every few seconds and "blasted" the onlookers who happened to walk by.

"Oh, I have got to see this," cried Mattie. He ran over to the booth, Jake calmly trailing behind him.

"I read about this in the convention guide," said Mattie. "There must be motion detectors built into it. Watch." He raised his hand, and the alien aimed at the movement. He stepped to his right, and it spun around, tracking him. "They must have paid a fortune to have this built. Man, just gimme a screwdriver and a couple of hours with this thing…."

Jake nodded, but his interest in the robot alien had already faded. His gaze fell on another part of the display. Without speaking, he tapped Mattie on the shoulder.

"Hmmm?"

"Check it out," said Jake.

Several pieces of original comic book artwork rested in an environmentally controlled, Lucite display case. The centerpiece, a pen-and-ink drawing on seventeen by twenty-two-inch illustration board, clearly identified itself as the most important work in the display. Below the words "Hero Comics" was an image of Hyperman lifting a car filled with escaping villains and smashing it nose-first against the side of a mountain. One of the villains was running away from the wreckage, his hands pressed to his face in dismay.

Jake stared, his mouth slightly open. "I don't believe it," he said. "That's Joe Sutter's original artwork for the cover of *Hero Comics #1*."

"The very first appearance of Hyperman," added Mattie.

The two stared at the image, neither of them speaking until several moments of quiet reverence had passed.

"Geez," said Jake. "A high-grade copy of the comic goes for over a hundred grand at auction. What do you suppose the original art is worth?"

"Oh, give it up," said Mattie. "It belongs in the Smithsonian."

As they spoke, a young man with a faintly familiar face strolled up to a nearby dealer booth. Jake could not place him immediately—he might have been in the line at the concession stand the day before, or a dealer at one of the tables Jake had browsed. He was dressed so shabbily, it seemed strange that he picked up some early Golden Age comics worth hundreds of dollars apiece.

Then Jake remembered…. *Dirty hair pulled back into a ponytail. T-shirt. Rumpled pants.*

It was the strange guy who had disappeared from the lecture hall just before the film was stolen. And here he was, looking dirty and destitute and holding probably five grand worth of vintage comics. It didn't necessarily mean anything, but it was a little weird. Jake wondered what might happen if he just tried to start up an innocent conversation.

"Mattie, wait here," he said. "I'll be right back."

The young man flipped slowly through the stack of comics. As Jake neared him, he glanced up. Jake's eyes met his, and their gazes locked. Then the young man handed the comics back to the dealer and very quickly walked away.

Jake decided to follow.

The young man moved down one of the aisles, motoring along like a tank, shouldering his way through the crowd. All the while, Jake followed at a distance. Jake thought for a moment that he had lost him, but then he looked to his right and saw the ponytail and the mud-gray T-shirt. The guy was fifteen or twenty yards ahead of Jake, cutting down a side aisle. He glanced over his shoulder, saw that Jake was following, and increased his speed. Then he broke into a run. Jake began to run as well, sidestepping children and twisting sideways to squeeze through groups of people, all the while keeping the man in sight.

The young man was just ahead of Jake—in fact, Jake was closing the distance between them—but the man was only a few yards away from the exit doors and the lobby. Jake knew that the greatest concentration of people was just beyond the doors. If the young man made it into the lobby, he could vanish. He could fade into the crowd, leave the convention center, and become just another person walking somewhere, anywhere, on the streets of downtown Bugle Point.

If Jake wanted to find out what this guy was up to, he had to do something—and quickly.

The young man slipped around another table, and Jake saw his chance. A box crammed with comics lay on the floor near the table, and Jake saw a way to cut the corner. He fell into an easy rhythm, and his foot hit the box of comics as though it were the first step on a staircase. He leaped from there to the top of the table, and from the table he leaped several feet into the air. It was a perfect flying tackle.

But things didn't go as Jake had planned. Out of the corner of his eye, the young man had seen Jake's leap, and he was ready. Instead of running into the path of Jake's tackle, he spun around, braced himself, and threw a forearm into Jake's chest. It struck right across the center of Jake's ribcage, knocking his legs out from under him and flipping him backward. He landed hard, smacking his head and shoulders against the linoleum floor. The young man fell as well, stumbling from the impact, but he recovered quickly. He scrambled to his feet and tore off through the exit doors.

His head still spinning, Jake heard the strangest sound—a faint, metallic ringing. He turned toward the sound and saw a quarter spinning on its edge, slowing, clinking to a rest on the floor. More coins lay scattered nearby—a few pennies, a nickel. They had fallen from young man's pocket when he stumbled.

And something else....

Jake drew himself to his knees and reached for a metal disk that lay among the coins. He held it up to the light, examined it, then stuck it in his pocket.

When he looked up, a man—the dealer who was working the table Jake had leaped from—stood over him, red-faced, holding a crumpled comic in his hand. "I hope you got ten bucks on you, kid," he said. "This comic's got your footprint all over the cover!"

Jake groaned. He stood, rubbed a hand over his sore back, and reached for his wallet.

Mattie was still waiting for him at the American Comics booth. Jake dragged himself over, giving a dismissive wave to the alien when it spun around and fired a few laser blasts at him.

"What happened to you?" asked Mattie. "You look halfway dead."

"Halfway's about right," Jake muttered. He reached into his pocket and pulled out the metallic disk. "That guy I was following? This fell out of his pocket when he…er…when he fell. Look familiar?"

He handed the disk to Mattie, and the younger boy stared at it, cupping it in his open palm. "Sure," he said. "It's a sound chip from an action figure." Set in the center of the disk was a small watch battery. Mattie touched his finger to a wire standing up from the disk, pressing it to the battery's edge.

The air filled with the insane laugh of the Jester.

Joe Sutter steered his wheelchair around his dining room table and rolled himself into the living room. On his way, he passed by the open door to the den. Even after all these years, Sutter felt a tightening in his chest, a twisting of the heart muscle every time he passed the room where he had created so much of his art. The drafting table was still there, covered with cloth.

Sometimes, for reasons he never really understood, he felt the need to look at the table, to remind himself what it had meant to him. He wheeled himself up to the table and tugged at the cloth, crumpling it in his lap.

The table was just as he remembered it—covered with flecks of india ink and scratches from his X-acto knife. Seeing these traces of his work brought back an odd memory: When Hyperman became a daily newspaper strip in 1942, Sutter began using an illustration board called Craftint. On the board were countless tiny black speckles, invisible until Sutter brushed a chemical developer over them. When he did, the speckles would darken, allowing him to create shades of gray in his black-and-white drawings. Strange. He hadn't thought of Craftint in years.

Sutter gazed at his brushes. So many inkers today used pens—pens! They were clean and easy to use, but the art they created was often flat and uninspiring. Sutter had always used brushes—messy, hard-to-handle brushes— but, oh, the line work you could create! Sutter's brushes had bristles of fine sable. He had always been so meticulous about them. Now they were dry and brittle, their fine, tapered points flared out like the tail of an angry cat. Useless.

He threw the cloth back over the table, hiding all those memories. There was no sense sitting there, especially if he was just going to get all misty-eyed over times that were long past.

He stopped at the pile of mail on the living room coffee table. It was always the same stuff: an occasional bill, advertising flyers to tell him what was on special at the grocery store, and those oversized brown envelopes telling him he may already hold the winning entry. The rest of the stack was personal correspondence—most of it from organizers of small-scale comic book conventions. They wanted to give their convention a big-time, national feel, and having a genuine, famous Golden Age artist like the creator of Hyperman was just what they needed.

The rest of the mail would be from fans—men in their forties who remembered reading Hyperman as children, children in their early teens hoping to get a "priceless" collectible. They all asked the same question: Would Sutter do a painting for them? Would he do a sketch? A few requested his autograph. The point was, everyone wanted something from him, and Joe Sutter was just tired of it all. Why should he care about these people? The Hyperman they wanted no longer existed—except in a painting on his living room wall. Sutter dropped the stack of mail in the trash can by his desk.

He reached for the remote control and turned up the volume on the TV. The satellite dish was a treasure, with its hundreds of channels. His forty-two-inch, wide-screen television. Surround-sound. Sutter liked that best of all. He could sit on the couch, crank up some space movie—he could never remember the titles—and marvel at the way the spaceships exploded *behind* him. He pressed the volume button again, and the living room vibrated with the sound of lasers or phasers or masers.

Sutter sat there, forcing himself to ignore the way the Hyperman painting seemed to stare back at him. The television image crowded everything else from his eyes, the booming sound crowded everything else from his ears, and Joe Sutter was almost able to forget about the past.

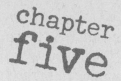
Friday evening

Charles Leach sat in a chair in his hotel room with his fist pressed against his chin. He was making a mental list of the things he still needed to do and the problems that needed to be solved before this business would be over.

Mercenary Comics always put their editors up in nice hotels during major comic book conventions, but Charles found this particular room to be, well, barely tolerable. The room was on the first floor, which Charles hated. The ground level view made him feel as though he were staying in a cheap motel. The current presence of Wilson A. Dominic didn't help matters either. Right now Dominic was sprawled across the bed, stuffing popcorn into his mouth, wrinkling the sheets, and planting who knows what forms of microbial life all over the pillowcases. Charles swallowed nervously and checked his watch. "It's eight-fifteen," he said. "The meeting was scheduled for eight o' clock. So where is the third member of our merry little band?"

Dominic tossed a piece of popcorn into the air and tried to catch it in his mouth. It ricocheted off his front teeth, landed on the floor, and rolled under the bed. Moaning, he hauled himself to the carpet and groped for it.

"Actually," said Charles, "I know what's happening. A streak of independence. You're too stupid to act on your own, Dominic, but our little friend is quite different in that regard."

"Don't call me stupid," warned Dominic, returning to the bed. "You need me. Without my help the film would be worthless to you, and you know it."

A twig crackled outside, and something skittered through leaves. Charles could see nothing through the room's window, but he stepped over to it and yanked it closed, shutting out the sounds and the cool wind. Dominic let out a laugh at Charles's alarmed expression.

"It was only a squirrel."

"Quiet!" said Charles, sitting again.

Dominic was right to laugh. Although Charles knew who was behind the Jester's mask—Charles, after all, had procured the costume and recruited the costume's wearer—there was still something eerie about seeing someone wearing the costume. It was like seeing the real Jester, face-to-face. The person wearing that mask seemed tall, strong, capable of *anything*. Worse, Charles sensed that the Jester understood the power of the costume and knew its psychological effect on others.

Charles rose from his chair. Standing made him feel a little more active, a little more in control. "Just wait until our friend shows up," he muttered. "I've got quite a few things to say."

The phone jangled, and Charles leaped for it. Catching himself at the last moment, he gripped the handset without lifting it, letting the phone ring a second time before picking it up.

"Yes?" he said into the phone.

"I'm altering the plan," said a voice. "I'm not coming to your hotel. Walk across the street to the convention center, and meet me in the main ballroom."

The voice hung up with a *click.*

Charles sat down, wiping his hand slowly across his mouth and chin as he pondered this turn of events. Then he rose quickly and grabbed his jacket from the closet. "Stay here," he said.

"Where're you going?" asked Dominic.

Charles punched his arms into the jacket sleeves. "To the convention center," he said. "It seems the Jester is trying to take charge of the operation."

Charles heard loud music as he approached the ballroom. Tonight was the costume party and the contest for best costume. When he entered, Charles saw that the bright lights in the ballroom had been replaced by colored spotlights swinging on tiny motors. A single, blinding strobe light flickered off and on, off and on, so that everyone on the ballroom floor seemed to move with an eerie stop-action effect.

And of course, there were the costumes. A few hundred people were on the dance floor, with perhaps two dozen of them costumed as the Jester. Here the Jester—*while wearing the costume*—could turn the film canisters over to Charles without creating the slightest suspicion. And what better way to unnerve Charles, to keep him off balance, than with the lights and the noise?

Charles's spine went cold.

—And the police.

They were barely visible, standing almost motionless at strategic points throughout the ballroom. Their navy blue uniforms melted into the blackness of the room's corners, leaving only the shiny brims of their hats—and the glitter of their badges—to catch the pulsing light from the strobe. Had there been only one or two, Charles might have assumed they were costumed partiers.

He counted fifteen.

Of course. After yesterday's robbery, the convention management would insist on added security for such a large crowd.

He eyed the police as he circled the outer edge of the dance floor and waited for the Jester—the right Jester—to come to him. He spent ten minutes doing just that, making two slow, complete trips around the room, steadying his pace and turning his head aside as he passed each officer. Inside, he boiled, hating the Jester all the more for luring him into this insane game of chicken.

Finally he heard a hoarse voice whisper, "Looking for someone?"

Charles spun around. It was the Jester. The dark purple of the villain's cape had blended with the shadows. Now, as the Jester moved closer, caught in the flickering effect from the strobe, Charles could see the frozen red smile on the mask.

Charles folded his arms limply in front of him, though even he sensed it was an unimpressive gesture. "Do you have everything?" he asked, a little too sharply.

The Jester held up a cloth bag. A drawstring held the bag closed, and the Jester tugged at it, opening the bag for just a instant, allowing Charles a glimpse of the canisters of film inside.

Charles smiled weakly. "Wonderful." He slung the bag over his shoulder, already forming a plausible story in his mind in case one of the police officers was bored enough to strike up a conversation: *Just visiting with a friend at the costume party. Now on my way for a little workout at the hotel gym, that's all.* Inside, his nerves began to settle a bit. In spite of the Jester's foolishness, the plan could still work. With his connections and Dominic's unique skill, they could produce copies of this movie for next to nothing and sell them for twenty or thirty dollars apiece. Ten thousand copies would bring them a minimum of two hundred thousand dollars.

"There is the matter of my…compensation," said the Jester, in that flat, muffled voice the mask produced.

"Quiet," said Charles, looking around. He calmed himself. The dance music was blaring. No one could hear them. "We agreed you'd get your share once the money began to come in."

"And there's something else," said the Jester evenly. "Setting off fireworks in the lecture hall was foolish. People could have been hurt. We agreed there would be no violence."

"I make the decisions around here," Charles snapped, but he could feel his lip quivering. "And by the way— regarding the clue you left after the job? That wasn't part of the scheme. From now on, you do what I say. I don't like it when someone departs from the plan. It's risky."

"I have a mind of my own, and I have my own reasons for doing what I do," the Jester said. "We had a bargain. I've held up my end of it. Just see that you live up to yours. And soon."

Charles affected a quick, forced laugh.

"When you give me my share of the money," the Jester said coldly, "our business arrangement is finished. I have my own plans, and they're none of your business."

The Jester stared at him with that gaping, plastic smile, then stepped back and melted into the shadows, leaving Charles with only the bag slung over his shoulder and the dreadful certainty that his plan had just been stolen from him.

Byte felt a shiver in her chest. She wasn't cold, just a little nervous.

She walked down the long hotel corridor, clutching her mother's gym bag and scanning the doors for room numbers. Her laptop hung from her shoulder in its case, and Byte held her elbow against it, pressing it to her body.

Getting permission to spend Friday night with Robin had been easier than Byte had anticipated. School wouldn't start again for two more days, so that was no problem. Byte's mom didn't mind driving her to the hotel, and Robin's father was staying in the next room. Most importantly, it wasn't as if the invitation was to a big party with guys and everything. Byte's mom said sure, she could go—as long as she at least checked in by e-mail.

Byte rapped lightly at the door of room 312. She heard a snapping sound, like suitcase latches, followed by a closet door closing, then the sound of feet padding across a carpet. Finally the door opened and Robin appeared, her face spreading into a smile.

"*Hiiii!*" Robin said, warmly extending the word into two or three syllables.

"Um, hi," said Byte.

Robin stepped back from the door and swung it open. "Come on in." She was holding a little magazine, a guide to the hotel's cable TV service, and she began fanning herself with it as Byte stepped into the room. "Whew," she said. "I'm warm. Does it seem too hot in here?"

Byte shook her head no.

"Oh, well. I guess I've been running around a lot today, with the convention and getting settled here and all."

Byte wasn't exactly sure what to say, so she said, "Yeah. Guess so."

After a long pause, Robin cleared her throat. "So," she said hesitantly, "you ever done this before?"

"You mean a slumber party? Uh-uh," said Byte. "You?"

Robin shook her head. "Nope." She plopped down on the floor in front of the television set, folded her legs beneath her, and gestured toward one of the beds. "Set your stuff down."

Byte nodded and lay the duffel bag on the floor next to the bed. Her computer bag, though, remained at her shoulder, her hand gripping the strap. A long, painful silence ensued.

"You're kind of a quiet person, huh," said Robin.

Byte nodded.

"That's cool," said Robin. "We should get along perfectly. People tell me that I talk too much. I have an opinion about everything, and I guess I sometimes forget that other people may not be interested in hearing it. Want to know what I think of liberal tax-and-spend policies?"

Byte started to speak, then closed her mouth, thinking that anything she said might set off a conversational land mine. Her mother was absolutely rabid about politics, and they sometimes talked about politics at home, but Byte hadn't exactly expected to be dealing with the subject at a slumber party. She remained silent, crinkling her nose to set her glasses straight.

Robin smiled. "Byte, I'm just kidding. Listen, I've been watching one of those political discussion shows on cable," said Robin. "Know what I'm going to do when I get out of high school?" She was beginning to talk even faster. "I'm going to go to pre-law at Harvard, then go to Harvard Law School, specialize in corporate law, make an obscene amount of money as a Washington, D.C., inside-the-Beltway attorney, and be a Supreme Court justice when I'm forty-two. I have it all planned."

Robin stopped to catch her breath. Byte, who was still trying to get her bearings in this conversation, could find nothing to say. She was beginning to get the impression that Robin was a person who, when a little nervous and unsure of what to say, runs off at the mouth like a fire hydrant with a broken valve.

Another moment of silence passed between them. Finally Robin pointed at the bag dangling from Byte's shoulder.

"Are you afraid I'm going to steal that?" she asked.

Byte looked down at the computer and chuckled, mostly at herself. "Nooo," she said, a little embarrassed. "I guess it's kind of a security blanket."

"So what is it?"

Byte smiled. Here was familiar territory. She unzipped the bag and took out her computer. "It's my laptop," she said. "I do all my schoolwork on it."

"*All* your work?" asked Robin.

"Uh-huh," said Byte. "It's like paper, pen, and note-book all rolled into one. I never take anything to class but this and my textbooks—and maybe a handout if the teacher gives us one."

"That's so *cool*," said Robin.

"Yeah," said Byte. "I even keep my diary on it. I can type faster than I can write, and my password is lots safer than those little locks they put on diary books. Here, I'll show you what it can do."

Byte opened up her computer, used the hotel phone to log on to her online provider, and in moments was on the Internet. She showed Robin the Harvard University Website, with its stately, gold logo. She entered the Website she herself had created for the science club at the high school, and she quickly browsed through two or three of her favorite chat rooms.

"Hey," Byte said, "let's see what the American Comics Website looks like."

Robin had been standing next to her, leaning over her shoulder to see the screen. Byte felt her stiffen. "Why are we going there?"

Byte looked at the expression on Robin's face—the flat-ness of her mouth, the angry set of her jaw—and suddenly began to see how much Robin resembled her grandfather.

"We don't have to," Byte said. "I just thought we might learn something, that's all. Jake said today he ran into a suspicious character from the screening, but I haven't come up with anything useful. We have no idea what the

Jester's up to next, and I'd love to find a clue that would help us figure all of this out."

The hard look remained on Robin's face a moment longer, then softened. She tilted her head first one way, then the other, playfully weighing the idea in her mind. "Okay," she said. "Let's take a look at it."

The menu page for the American Comics Website featured Hyperman, of course, in an image taken from the cover of an upcoming hardcover graphic novel. Hyperman stood slightly hunched, his neck, shoulder, and chest muscles tensed, and he was grimacing like a body-builder in pose. Byte went straight to the menu buttons.

"Let's see," she said, "New Releases…Hyperman Movie Info…Who's Who—oh, let's look at that."

The Who's Who section of the Website consisted of biographical information about the artists, writers, and editorial staff at American Comics. "I'm just wondering who we might talk to," said Byte. "Several of these people are bound to be at the convention." Small color photographs accompanied most of the bios, and Byte quickly scanned each one. One man in particular seemed to glare at her from the screen, a dark-haired man with sunken cheeks and a black patch over his left eye. "Here are the artists who are working on the Hyperman comics," said Byte. "Yikes, who's this guy?"

"That's Adrian Bock," said Robin. "I read his interview in *Wizard* magazine. He's in his mid-twenties and new to the Hyperman titles—not likely to know a lot of inside stuff."

84   Bock's biographical sketch was brief—a mention of his birthplace, the art college he attended, and one or two artists he listed as influences. Byte saw none of the humor, warmth, or chattiness she found in some of the other biographies. She imagined Bock angrily scribbling these few words and tossing them onto his editor's desk.

"Well, that doesn't tell us much," said Byte. "How about the editor?"

"Just moved to American Comics from another publisher," said Robin. "AC's been 'revamping' Hyperman, if you hadn't noticed. They've brought in whole new creative teams."

Seeing that she had covered everyone who was working specifically on Hyperman—and learned little—Byte exited from the Website and shut down her computer. She turned to find Robin smiling at her.

"Hey, Byte, thanks for showing me all that. Especially the Harvard stuff."

"Any time," said Byte.

Robin moved quickly over to one of the beds and landed on it with a bounce. "Okay," she said, reaching for the telephone, "now for something really important. What do you like on your pizza?"

Byte smiled. "Onions. Lots of onions."

Half an hour later, after the pizza arrived, the two changed into pajamas, and Robin clicked through the cable stations looking for a horror movie.

"Here we go," she said. "*Scream 2*. Seen it?"

Byte, her mouth full of pizza, nodded.

Robin thought for a moment. "You know what I'm wondering?" she said. "Neve Campbell's character in the movie—she's been chased twice now, right? Twice some crazies have tried to kill her?"

Byte nodded.

"I keep thinking—well, come on, girl, why don't you move to *Nebraska* or something?"

Byte stared at Robin, and the two girls burst out laughing.

A little while later the empty, grease-spotted pizza box lay open on the hotel room desk. The movie came to a particularly illogical moment, and Robin dropped her slice of pizza onto a paper plate in disgust. "Okay," she said, "enough of this. It's brutal honesty time. We're two girls having a sleepover; it's absolutely required that we talk about guys. It's in the slumber party contract." She grinned evilly and pointed at Byte. "You first."

Byte's eyes narrowed. "Wait a minute," she said, "this is a two-way deal, right?"

"Of course," said Robin. "I'll go right after you. Maybe. If I feel like it. No—wait wait wait." She waved her hands, erasing everything she had just said. "I have a better idea. You don't have to tell me. I'll guess." She placed two fingers against her forehead and stared at Byte, looking every bit like a sideshow mind reader. "Hmmm…yes, the clouds are clearing…I see a very tall boy…gorgeous bod…his name is…*Jake Armstrong!*"

"*Noooo!*" Byte turned red, then near-purple. She put her hand up to her face to hide herself behind her fingers. "Oh, this is so embarrassing," she said, laughing.

She pointed a threatening finger at Robin. "You'd better not tell. I'll die if you tell."

Robin held up three fingers in a scouting salute, a single eyebrow arched playfully. "I won't tell," she said. "Scout's honor." Then she leaned in and whispered, "Of course, I was never a Scout."

Byte grabbed a cushion from the chair and smacked Robin with it.

Robin laughed. "Just *kidding.*"

"All right, then," Byte said. "I bet I know who *you're* after. Peter, right?" She sat back with her hands joined behind her head, beaming.

"I don't believe it," Robin said incredulously. "It can't be that obvious."

"Oh, Peter doesn't have a clue," said Byte, "but I could tell. That's why you invited us to the convention, isn't it? You were going to be here all weekend, and you wanted to spend some time with Peter."

Robin leaned back and smirked. "Okay, then," she said, "if you're so smart, why did I wait until now? Peter and I have been in classes together off and on since the sixth grade."

"That's easy," said Byte. "It's the comic connection. You somehow picked up that Jake and Mattie are comic fanatics. You also knew that we all hang out with Peter. So, the Comicon is the mousetrap, the guest badges are the cheese, Jake and Mattie are the mice, and you knew if you could lure them there, Peter would come, too. Of course, you could have done it sooner—cooked up a study date or something—but I figure it probably took you this long to admit to *yourself* that you like Peter. He does take some getting used to."

Robin laughed at Byte's description, then looked at the ceiling and shook her head. "I can't believe I'm admitting this. Peter and I have been at each other's throats for as long as I can remember. He had a higher g.p.a.; I made Honor Society. He won the eighth-grade chess tournament, then I made captain of the debate team. It's been like that since sixth grade. Back and forth. He wins, then I win. The score is tied, and the guy I like hates me."

Byte paused a moment. "That's a pretty shallow opinion of Peter, I think," she said. "Peter doesn't hate you. He just doesn't like it very much when you come out ahead of him in competition. It's his ego."

Robin shrugged, seemingly unsure about whether or not she believed Byte. Distracted by the television, she glanced at the screen and saw that Neve Campbell was screaming again. "Isn't she dead yet?"

She dragged herself over to the bed and scooped up a deck of playing cards that were laid out in a solitaire hand. She sat across from Byte, shuffled, and began dealing, the number of cards indicating the game she had chosen: SPIT.

"I know about your group," Robin said, snapping a card off the deck. "The circle/square symbol and all that. How did that come about?"

Byte considered the question for a moment. "The symbol was Peter's idea. I got to be friends with Peter when the two of us tried out for the drama production. Then we became friends with Jake, and later Mattie became part of the group."

"*You* tried out for drama?"

"Hey, you have to have an art credit to graduate, and I can't draw. Peter and I managed to turn in the worst audition ever seen in the history of the drama program at Bugle Point High School. I was stiff as a stick up there, and Peter, I don't know…. We were auditioning for a Neil Simon play, and he acted like it was Shakespeare. We were awful. The second we finished, Mrs. Scapelli asked if one of us was interested in operating the light board."

"That's a bad sign," said Robin.

"You're telling me! But that's how Peter and I got to be friends. Later in the year, right after spring break, this jerk in the junior class started picking on me, calling me a geek and things like that—and Peter stood up for me."

"That's so chivalrous," said Robin. "Like a knight on a horse. What did the guy do?"

Byte stifled a laugh. "He gave Peter a black eye."

"Peter got a black eye for you?"

"Yup."

Robin sighed. "Nothing cool like that ever happens to me." She turned over a card, a jack: "Ready? Spit!"

The two girls immediately began slamming down cards from their hands, snapping each card on top of the last, trying to get rid of everything they held. The scattered pile grew, quickly moving from the jack all the way down to a three, which Byte smacked on top of the pile.

"Unless you have a two...." she said.

Robin fanned out the cards in her hand. The lowest one remaining was a seven.

"Look," said Byte, as Robin gathered up the cards for another round, "don't worry about Peter. He respects you a lot."

"I'm not so sure...." said Robin.

"I am," said Byte. "You want me to ask him?"

"Byte!" Robin shrieked.

Byte smirked. "Just kidding!"

chapter
six

Saturday

the following morning Byte and Robin awoke early. They threw on some warm clothes, ate muffins and drank orange juice in the plush hotel dining room, and walked outside toward the convention center, shivering as the wind whipped their hair about their faces.

"I've been thinking about something," said Byte.

They stopped at the intersection and waited for the light to change. Robin gazed off, seemingly distracted. "Hmmm?"

"It's different talking to you. I've known Peter, Jake, and Mattie for a while—and we're really close—but someone would have to torture me before I'd tell the guys *half* the stuff we talked about last night."

"What?" said Robin. "You wouldn't talk to Mattie about how intense Jake looks when he's thinking? And how he doesn't talk much, but you can tell he's really deep?" She danced around Byte, swooning like a silent movie star. "And how you'd like to really understand him?"

Byte laughed despite herself. "Okay, okay—enough already!"

She had spent a great deal of the night thinking, and by the time she and Robin walked through the doors of the convention center, Byte had made a decision. "Hey, listen," she said. "I've got something I have to do. I'll catch up with you in a few minutes, okay?"

Robin shrugged. "That's fine. I should check in with my dad anyway. I'll see you later."

"Okay."

Byte headed toward the section of the convention floor set aside for the publisher booths. The publishers—more than any other group at the comic convention—seemed intent on outdoing one another with their displays. The AC booth, with its resident robot alien, was one of the easier ones to spot from a distance.

There it is, thought Byte as she walked toward it. *American Comics. The company that owns Hyperman.* She took stock of the booth's inhabitants. *Okay, who do I approach?* She scanned the faces of the people at the booth.

Oh!...

Seated at the booth, sullen and scowling as he signed autographs, was Adrian Bock. A line of fans—all males, ranging in age from about twelve to twenty-five—stood in front of him. As each approached with a sheet of paper, autograph book, or comic, Bock yanked it from the fan's fingers and scribbled a signature. If the fan asked for a sketch, Bock would gesture to the end of the table. "Forty bucks," he would say. "Wait there. It'll be half an hour."

Seated near Bock was a blond woman. Her squared shoulders and straight back let Byte know she was in charge.

Byte walked up to her and nervously offered a handshake. "Hello," she said. "My name is Byte Salzmann. Excuse me, but—are you an editor or something?"

"Hello," said the woman, taking Byte's hand. Her half-hearted smile suggested that, after two full days of talking with fans, the woman's patience was a bit strained. "I'm Janine Cook," she said. "I'm the publisher. What can I do for you?"

Byte swallowed. The publisher? This woman *was* important. "Well," said Byte, "I wanted to talk to you about Joe Sutter."

Janine Cook looked up at Byte, her eyes running back and forth over Byte's features. The woman paused for a very long moment before responding. "Well," she finally said, "that's not a subject that comes up very often. Are you with the press?"

Byte flushed at the question. How could someone look at a skinny teenage girl and see a journalist? Then she remembered the computer bag at her shoulder.

"Ohhh," said Byte, understanding. "No, this is just my laptop. I never know when I might need it."

The woman nodded slowly. Byte hoped she hadn't just blown any chance she'd had of getting some straight answers.

"So," the woman said, "what about Joe Sutter? There's a very fine Hyperman museum here at our booth. The original costume from the 1950s Hyperman TV series is on display, there's some original artwork, and you can see a short film we've made about Mr. Sutter and his partner."

"No, thank you," said Byte. "I guess I wanted to talk to you about what Joe Sutter has done for the comic book industry." She paused. "And what I think the industry ought to be doing for him."

Bock, overhearing Byte's remark, shot a glance in her direction. She caught him just as he turned his head away, and she heard him muttering under his breath. Amid the vague grumbling, Byte made out the words *Sutter, artwork,* and, strangely, *I'll show them. Show them all....*

Janine Cook glared at the artist, and the muttering stopped.

What will happen now? Byte wondered. *Will the woman dismiss me, or at best, give me generic answers written by an attorney?* Adrian Bock silently continued to sign autographs, and Janine Cook looked carefully at Byte. Finally, the publisher tossed down her pen, stood, and hung her blazer across the back of a chair. "Let's go somewhere else to talk," she said, striding away from the booth.

"Tell me, Byte—why such an interest in Joe Sutter?"

Walking across the convention floor, Byte forgot the

costumed convention shoppers and the eager sales-people for a moment. She had a sudden flash of Mr. Sutter sitting in his wheelchair. "Um, his granddaughter is a friend of mine. He's—he's very bitter. And I think he has a right to be."

"Oh?"

"Well, yeah," Byte continued. "I mean, Hyperman has made millions of dollars since Mr. Sutter created him, but Mr. Sutter doesn't get any of the money. It isn't fair."

They passed the concession area, where vendors at wagon carts offered hot pretzels, donuts and muffins, and coffees and cappuccinos. Janine Cook led Byte to the coffee vendor. "Do you drink coffee?" she asked. "I'm buying."

"Sure," said Byte. "Thanks." Actually, Byte had only tried coffee once or twice in her life, but right now it seemed appropriate to accept the offer.

"As you may know," said Ms. Cook, placing a five-dollar bill on the counter, "there's been some unplanned excitement here at the convention. Someone stole a print of the new Hyperman movie."

"The Jester," said Byte.

Janine Cook raised an eyebrow. "You saw it?"

"My friends and I practically had front row seats."

"I see," said the publisher. "At any rate, your mentioning Joe Sutter set off a few alarms. His story is a sensitive subject right now, and with everything that's going on—the theft and the upcoming release of the film—it's become even more sensitive. You understand why, don't you?"

Byte nodded. "I think so. It's because Hunter Brothers Studios is the parent company of American Comics. With all this attention on the Hyperman movie, the press might do some stories on Hyperman and on American Comics' treatment of Joe Sutter. That would make American Comics look bad, and people might not go see the Hunter Brothers film."

"Exactly," said the publisher. "The Hyperman film was an eighty-million-dollar investment, and it's just the beginning. Remember when you talked about the merchandising money Hyperman has generated over the years? You said millions. Actually, the figure is closer to a billion—that's since the early 1940s. And it's growing all the time. Toy Buzz just paid us a hefty licensing fee for a new line of Hyperman action figures to tie in with the film."

Byte felt a pang for Joe Sutter. "But isn't Mr. Sutter entitled to *any* of that money? I did some Web surfing and found a little information on the history of the comic business. Joe Sutter made the modern comic book industry possible. Until he came along, comic books were nothing—just reprints of the Sunday funnies. The first appearance of Hyperman changed all that."

The publisher didn't say anything for a while. She twirled the stirrer in her coffee cup and seemed to lose herself in the swirling liquid. "Well," she finally said, "I guess there's a lot of truth in that. However, if I were to give you the corporate line in response to your question,

I would have to say no. Joe Sutter and Barry Nagel legally signed their rights over to us. The courts have ruled to that effect on a number of occasions."

"But—"

"Wait," Janine said, "let me finish. That's the corporate response. That's what I'm supposed to say. The problem is—and what I'm about to tell you does not go beyond this table—I sometimes have a tough time believing it's right."

Byte looked at the woman, surprised that Janine Cook would show this much compassion. Was she sincere, or was this lecture a setup for some well-rehearsed brush-off?

"You have to understand something, Byte," said the publisher. "Like most of the people who work in comics, I got into the field because I love the medium. I've been a science fiction and comic book fan my whole life—Batman, *Star Trek*, everything. I went to all the conventions."

Byte smiled. "Did you wear rubber pointed ears?"

The publisher laughed. "Are you kidding? The ears were part of the uniform." She paused, drawing her finger along the edge of her coffee cup as she thought. "Byte, comic books are entirely different now than they were in Joe Sutter's time. Back then, they were cartoons drawn for the ten-year-old boy who would buy them at a neighborhood newsstand, sit down and read them at the curb, then ride home on his bicycle with the comics rolled up in his back pocket. Now most comic buyers are between the ages of eighteen and thirty-four, and for the most part the stories and art have grown more sophisticated to meet that audience. So the medium I loved as a little girl I can *still* love as a grown woman. Did you know, Byte, that a few years ago a comic book—a *comic book!*—won a Hugo award for best fantasy short story?"

Byte smiled. "My friend Jake told me about that. The other writers were so enraged that they forced the awards committee to change the rules so a comic book could never win again."

"Yes. We published that comic book, and I take great pride in it." Janine Cook crumpled her napkin and dropped it to the table. "Listen, Byte," she said, "on a personal level, and totally off the record, I agree with you about Joe Sutter. The industry owes him. It's just that, even as publisher, I'm not the final decision-maker at AC. Something like this goes right up the ladder to the parent company. I can't just whip out a checkbook and make the man's life better."

"Somebody should," said Byte.

Janine Cook nodded. "Yes, maybe someone should. I've pitched ideas here and there, but I'm afraid things won't change unless there's a way to convince the higher-ups that passing a bundle along to Joe Sutter will somehow improve their own bottom line."

"I just wanted to help the man," Byte murmured, more to herself than to the publisher. "I wanted to make things right for him."

"I know," said Janine. "That's why we're having this conversation. If I thought you were acting as Sutter's agent, or that you were a reporter looking for a story, I would have done my lawyer routine and hustled you off."

Janine Cook stood then and dropped her empty Styrofoam cup into a nearby trash can. "I'd better get back to the booth," she said. "The crew might be in mutiny." She reached out her hand, and Byte clasped it. "You seem to be a good person, Byte," she said. "If you get any ideas about how I can make a realistic pitch on Joe Sutter's behalf, you come see me, okay?"

Byte nodded, and Janine Cook began to leave.

"Oh—Ms. Cook?" called Byte.

The woman stopped and faced her.

"Tell me if this is none of my business, but what's the story with Adrian Bock? What's his problem?"

Janine Cook's face reddened, then very slowly returned to its natural paleness. "He's an artist," she said, as though that explained everything. "Actually, he's very passionate about artist issues in the industry—you know, fighting for artists' rights and such. He's also a big supporter of Joe Sutter."

Without another word, the woman turned and left.

For several minutes, Byte sat at the table, alone with her thoughts. Even though Janine Cook had been much nicer than she had expected her to be, Byte still hadn't gotten anywhere. All she had learned was that her idea of the villain in this matter might have to undergo some adjustment.

And she had also learned that the Misfits needed to have a little chat with Adrian Bock.

She took a sip of her coffee, made a face, and dumped the cup into the trash can.

Half an hour later Byte found Peter at one of the dealer booths, gazing at a 1966 tin Hyperman robot from Japan. The vintage toy was still in its original—though tattered—box, the Hyperman logo swooping across the front in Japanese lettering.

"Two hundred bucks," said the dealer.

Byte clamped a hand down on Peter's shoulder, crumpling the fabric of his T-shirt in her fist and pulling him away from the table. "Come on," she said. "I want to question someone right away, and I need your brain."

She led him to a spot a few dozen yards from the AC booth. The two of them stood where main aisles formed a juncture. Crowds filtered past them, effectively hiding them from the occupants of the booth.

"See the blond woman?" said Byte, pointing to Janine Cook. "We have to wait until she leaves."

The publisher obliged them a few moments later, when she checked her pager and strode off, apparently in search of a phone.

"Now," said Byte. "Just follow my lead."

The autograph lines had diminished considerably since Byte had last been at the booth. She and Peter waited only a few minutes before they were at the head of the line and standing before the artist with the eye patch. Though seated, Adrian Bock appeared to be quite small;

he was thin, his features sharp and almost birdlike beneath his mass of curly black hair.

Without raising his head to look at them, Bock grabbed a sheet of paper from Peter's fingers, scribbled his autograph on it, and thrust it back.

Peter stared at it dully. "Um, that was my map of the dealer room floor."

Byte edged a little closer to Peter. "Excuse me, Mr. Bock," she blurted out, "but we were wondering if we could ask you a couple of questions about Joe Sutter."

At the mention of the name, Adrian Bock finally raised his head. He stared at Peter and Byte, and his hands slowly drew together, his long, delicate fingers steepling beneath his nose.

"Yes?"

"Well, I mean," said Byte, "what do you think of his situation?"

Byte was going to say more, but Adrian Bock suddenly slammed both his palms down on the tabletop. The sound echoed and the table shook. One of the other artists—who had just scribbled an errant line across a piece of artwork he was finishing for a fan—glared at Bock and told him to knock it off.

"His *situation?*" said Bock. "What do I think of his *situation?*" Byte got the point: "situation" was too much of an understatement, too weak and unfair a description of Joe Sutter's plight. "I'll tell you what I think," said Bock. "I think the industry ought to get on its collective knees and pay homage to Joe Sutter. I think they ought to build pyramids to honor his name. Instead, they take his creation, milk it for every dime, and laugh at him all the way to the bank!"

His anger took Byte by surprise. She took half a step backward, as though Bock's words were solid objects she had to dodge.

"They should suffer, do you hear me?" Bock shouted. "The industry took advantage of its artists for decades—wallpapering their offices with original artwork, then tossing it all in the trash when they tired of it!" He pounded on the table again. This time, his fellow artist threw down his pen and handed the near-complete drawing to the fan, telling him he could have it free of charge.

Byte saw Peter tense. He had apparently figured out why they were speaking to Bock.

"Mr. Bock," said Peter, "can you tell us where you were around 10:30 Thursday morning?"

Bock hesitated, either confused by the question or unnerved by having to give an answer; Byte could not tell which. But then the artist leaned forward, smiling. His lips peeled back into a leer, and he began to chuckle. His thin, clawlike fingers made a broad, expansive gesture across the dealer room floor.

"Right here," he said, indicating the huge, crowded space before him, "with a line of fifty people waiting for my autograph."

It was almost lunchtime when Robin and the Misfits met to talk about the Jester. The group sat on a grassy area just outside the convention center entrance. It was chilly outdoors, but it was easier to hear one another than it was indoors, with thousands of people crowded around.

"The ponytailed guy *has* to be involved," said Jake. He and Mattie had spoken to the others the day before about the man Jake had chased and the sound chip of the Jester's laugh. "He might even be the Jester. Why else would he run?"

"And this Adrian Bock guy gives me the creeps," added Byte. "Alibi or not, he's still a suspect in my book. Maybe he and your ponytailed guy are working together."

"They're both suspects," said Peter. "Good work tracking them down. While you guys were busy, I tried to figure out the clue and the Jester's next move. Whoever the Jester is, I think he'll be striking again tonight—sometime after eight o'clock. The dealer room will be empty all night long."

"But how can you be sure the theft is going to be tonight?" asked Robin.

Peter reached into his pocket and removed the napkin on which Mattie had jotted the Jester's riddle. "I've been thinking about that," he said. "Listen…."

> *On Saturn's eve, in darkness' smoke,*
> *A tale to tell, a whisper spoke,*
> *An old man's trial, the Jester's smile,*
> *Now turn upon a hero's cloak.*

"Remember when we studied the epics in English?" said Peter. "Saturn was one of the Roman gods. The god of crops or something."

"Agriculture," corrected Robin.

"Um, right," Peter said, shaking off his annoyance. "Anyway, I remembered that Saturn had a day of the week named after him."

"Saturday," said Byte.

Peter nodded. "Exactly. So the Jester will be striking tonight."

Robin looked unimpressed. "Or not," she said. "Saturn's *eve* could be like Christmas Eve, as in the night before. The clue could be talking about *Friday* night. Maybe he's already done whatever he's going to do, and we just haven't heard about it yet."

Peter shook his head. "I don't think so. The Jester likes daring crimes and flashy effects. If he'd made an appearance last night, we'd know about it. Anyway, all that was scheduled for last night was the costume party, and there wasn't anything there to steal. I think the Jester will be trying to make off with something big again, and I think he'll do it on the last night of the convention. It'll be his grand finale."

"Okay," said Jake, "so the Jester strikes tonight. But *how?* What's he going to steal next?"

Peter hesitated. There were hundreds of thousands of expensive collectibles in that dealer room, any one of which might attract the Jester. The Misfits couldn't possibly watch everything.

"I don't know," said Peter. "I haven't been able to figure that out. The thief is obviously interested in things pertaining to Hyperman."

"That helps some, but not much," said Jake. "Because of the movie, half the dealers here brought their best Hyperman stuff. I've seen rings, premiums from old cereal boxes, vintage wristwatches, and stacks of artwork."

"Okay, so we need to narrow down the list of potential targets," Mattie said. "What are the biggest Hyperman-related items at the convention?"

The group remained thoughtful and quiet, the sounds from the convention floor a distant rumbling behind them.

"Well," Byte said, breaking their silence, "AC set up a little Hyperman museum. They're displaying an original costume from the old Hyperman TV show."

"Hey," said Jake, "and the Jester was wearing the Golden Age outfit. Maybe he's into old costumes."

"And Adrian Bock certainly knows how much attention the costume's been getting," Byte murmured. "He's been sitting right next to it in the AC booth for over two days."

Robin thought for a moment, then her voice rose with excitement. "That's right!" she shouted, pointing to the riddle on the napkin. "The costume has to be it! A 'hero's cloak,' see?"

"It works," said Jake.

"That *has* to be it," said Mattie.

Peter was uncertain. "I don't know," he said. "That's one possibility, but there's a lot riding on this. Maybe we should look at some other—"

"Oh come *on,* Braddock," said Robin. "It's not like we have all day to sit around talking about it. You know I'm right. It's the most likely option, and we have to gamble." She crossed her arms, challenging him with a single raised eyebrow. "You're just upset because you didn't think of it yourself."

Peter, wounded, for once could think of nothing to say.

Out on the convention floor, Charles Leach had finally reached a point where he would just as soon cut off his right hand as pass out another promotional item.

He took a promo comic from the stack of freebies and passed it to an unshaven, scruffy-haired fan. Then he sighed wearily.

At least Dominic was standing near the head of the line. If nothing else, the guy was prompt. Charles glanced at his watch. It was 4:30, the exact time he had ordered Dominic to meet him. Suddenly Charles was grateful for the crowds at this convention. So many people attended the Bugle Point Comicon, it seemed unlikely that his fellow employees would notice that the same person kept showing up in Charles's line. At a smaller show, Dominic's reappearances would not have seemed so random.

When Dominic approached the table, Charles opened the comic book and began scribbling.

There's been a slight change of plan.

Dominic read the words, straining to make them out from his upside-down perspective. Then he nodded, covering the gesture by pretending to wipe his nose at the same time.

I know what our friend is up to. Meet me at the hotel to discuss. 7:00 P.M.

Dominic wiped his nose again, took the comic, and trudged off into the crowd.

Charles leaned back in his chair and smiled. Most people would not be able to solve the Jester's clue—but unlike most people, Charles knew the face behind the mask. Maybe the Jester's independence wasn't such a bad development after all, he decided. With some care and a little bit of preparation, Charles would possess *another* prize.

He thought of the nervousness, the fear he had shown at seeing the Jester in costume. He would win this battle of wills, he vowed, and he would make the Jester pay for humiliating him.

chapter seven

the dealer room had closed hours ago. The lights were off, and the acres of silent space had taken on the look and feel of a giant cavern. As the moon rose and shone through the skylights, everything in the room took on a pale blueness—the walls, the ceiling, even the covers of the few comic books still on display. Many of the vendors had packed their more expensive wares and carried them off to their hotel rooms. The empty display racks, looming in the darkness, looked like wiry skeletons.

Peter, crouching in the shadows, heard something rustling behind him. "Shhh," he said.

"I can't help it," whispered Mattie. "I'm getting a cramp in my leg."

Robin had arranged, without her father's knowledge, to sneak the Misfits onto the convention center floor. A stolen key, a few flirty moments between Robin and a distracted young security guard, and the Misfits had slipped inside. Now they hid perhaps fifteen yards from the American Comics booth. Inside the booth's inter-locking, prefabricated walls was an enormous glass showcase, and inside the showcase was a treasure—the original costume from the 1950s Hyperman TV show. Unlike most of the comic shop owners attending the convention, American Comics could afford a high-security showcase made of unbreakable glass. Only the major publishers left their most valuable items here overnight.

The only guard was the security officer from earlier, who stood several hundred yards away, guarding the entrance from the outside.

Mattie tugged at Byte's jacket. "Hey," he whispered, "where's Robin the Girl Wonder? I figured she'd want to be in on this."

Byte moved closer to Mattie. "She couldn't. Tonight's the night they announce the Eagle Award winners. Her dad insisted they attend the dinner, the awards presenta-tion, and the dance afterwards."

"Great," hissed Jake, "we get to crouch in a dark room for five hours, and she gets to listen to Seduction of the Innocent."

"Are they playing tonight?" asked Mattie.

"Yup," said Jake.

"And we're *missing* them?"

Peter sighed. "C'mon, guys," he whispered, "keep it down."

Peter tried to focus his attention on the job at hand. He had chosen the hiding place with great care. To steal the costume, Peter figured, the Jester would most likely make his way down from the catwalk, creep right past the Misfits, and somehow get into that monster display case. When he turned to escape, he would find the Misfits cutting off his only path.

"Hey, Mattie," said Byte, "I've been wondering. In the comic book, when people try to catch the Jester, what happens to them?"

Mattie shrugged. "In the Silver Age, from around the mid-1950s to the mid-1960s, the Comics Code Authority started 'approving' all the comic books. They turned the Jester into a big clown. His crimes were like pranks or jokes. No one got hurt."

"And before then?" asked Byte. "In the Golden Age?"

"Oh, in the Golden Age," said Mattie, "he was a homicidal maniac. He fired a gas at his victims that made them laugh until their brains exploded. Then they'd have this panel where maybe the eyeballs would be rolling across the floor like marbles or something."

"That's so *cool*," said Jake. "I *love* the pre-code books!"

"Okay, okay," Byte said. "And which costume did you say *our* Jester was wearing?"

"The Golden Age one."

"Great," grumbled Byte. "Just great."

They waited another hour, crouched in almost absolute silence. The only sounds were Jake's occasional shifting of weight and Mattie's griping about missing the band.

110   A little before 11:00, they heard the creak of a vent being opened near the catwalk. It made very little sound, just a light squeal, but in the silence of the dealer room it was as sharp as a rifle crack. Footsteps tapped on the walkway, then down the staircase. A shadow formed. Maybe it was just a trick of the moonlight, but the shadow looked *big*.

"This is it, Pete," whispered Jake. "We've got him."

The shadow moved toward the AC booth. Peter heard a tiny clicking sound, and a flashlight cast a pool of light on the floor. The person holding the flashlight cupped a hand around the lens so the beam wouldn't flicker against the walls.

The shadow drew closer, became more defined, then separated into *two* shadows. *What's this?* Peter wondered. *In the comics, the Jester always works alone.*

The two people drew closer to the Misfits' hiding place.

"Get ready," whispered Peter.

He was so busy following the movement of the glowing hand, he almost missed a flicker of motion from the opposite side of the AC booth. Something dark was moving over there as well. Peter heard a rustle of clothing.

What's going on?

Two people seemed to be approaching the booth from one direction, and a third person was approaching from another. *What's happening here? Are there two sets of thieves? Two Jesters? Or has someone besides us solved the riddle?*

The Jester—or Jesters—were not heading for the glass showcase containing the costume. They were all moving toward the far end of the booth, away from the Misfits' hiding place.

Peter's mouth hardened into a thin line. "We've been had," he whispered. "They're not here for the costume after all. Quick—what's over there?"

Jake's words hissed in Peter's ear. "Oh, no! It's Joe Sutter's original artwork to the cover of *Hero Comics #1*."

This trio of criminals had fooled them. Now the Misfits were out of position, no longer able to cut off the path of escape.

"What do we do?" Mattie whispered frantically. "We have to stop them!"

The shadow closest to the AC booth stepped into a patch of moonlight, and Peter was able to make out a face. It was indeed the Jester. Peter saw the hood, the cape, and that awful, grinning mask. Worse, the Jester was staring right at the Misfits, as though the villain knew they were hiding there. The Jester reached to his belt, raised a flashlight, and clicked on the beam.

Then Peter heard the laughter—loud, shrieking, and utterly insane.

In an eye blink the Jester raised a hand to the "robber-proof" frame over the artwork, seemed to jiggle it, and, amazingly, the frame popped off the wall. Peter knew they could no longer wait for the Jester to come to them. *For Joe Sutter, and for Robin, we have to do something—*

"Now!" whispered Peter. "Let's get him!"

Jake was the first to leap from the hiding place. Since the Jester already had his hands on the artwork, the Misfits ignored the other two shadows and concentrated on him. The Jester, suddenly faced with four bodies sprinting in his direction, dropped his flashlight, grabbed the artwork, and ran. He vanished into the darkness, his cape whipping behind him.

"He'll head toward the catwalk!" yelled Peter. "Cut him off!"

Because the Misfits were out of position, the Jester had a head start and therefore a good chance of making it to the catwalk ahead of them. As Peter looked on, the Jester raced closer to the two shadows lurking just beyond the far end of the AC booth, seemingly unaware of their presence.

Even in the darkness, Peter could see one of the shadows raise a flashlight, and before the Jester could take another step it arced downward like a club. Arm, fist, and flashlight caught the Jester across the chest and slammed him to the floor. The framed artwork crashed to the ground, showering the floor with glass.

The flashlight trained itself on the Jester, then on the Misfits, who had stopped running, then on the artwork on the floor. Hands with thick fingers dipped into the pool of light and lifted the picture from the broken frame. Peter could just make out a bulky shape in a black sweatshirt, and he could hear the figure grunting as it bent over.

"Careful," said a voice, its tone edged with contempt. "Don't let the glass cut the artwork."

Peter watched the Jester roll onto his back, and it was clear that the villain was more than a little bruised from the fall he had taken. It seemed likely to Peter that the Misfits were witnessing a falling out among a single group of thieves.

"You're not taking that," Peter said. "There are four of us. We won't let you get away." In spite of his tough words, his voice cracked as he spoke.

"Oh, I think you will," came the reply. The voice was high-pitched and abrasive, like rocks scraping together.

Peter heard another sound and recognized it all too well. It was a slide drawing back on a semi-automatic pistol, followed by the click of a bullet entering the chamber. He had been around his father's weapons enough to know.

"Are you crazy?" said the other voice in the darkness. "What are you doing with that?"

The first voice whined again. "I'm taking care of things!" it said. "We don't need any witnesses."

"Hey, *wait*," Peter said quickly. "We're not witnesses! We can't even see you."

The abrasive voice laughed. "Maybe not," it whined, "but the Jester is a different story."

"What?" said the second voice. "You can't just shoot someone. That's insane!"

The shadowy figure raised a gun and held it at arm's length, elbow locked, aiming at the Jester.

The first voice spoke again. "No witnesses…and no sharing the wealth."

The Jester was still on the floor, on his back, and Peter's heart pounded as he watched the villian creep backward, spider-like, away from the danger.

The only sound was a *click* as the bulky figure cocked the gun.

Mattie watched the scene before him. Crouching low, he backed slowly away and bumped into something. When he looked up, he saw a seven-foot-tall alien staring down at him. Of course. The alien guard. With the ray gun.

And built-in motion detectors.

Mattie moved closer and felt along the alien's back until he found a plastic toggle switch. When he flicked it on, green lights flashed in the alien's eyes and a red glow spread across the tip of the ray gun. Mattie then reached behind him to the table where the AC marketing team had placed a box containing Hyperman promo buttons. *Let's hope the flashlight's bright enough for this to work.*

He grabbed the entire box and tossed it into the air, aiming as best he could for the gunman. The buttons scattered, a mass of shiny metal circles glinting in the flashlight's beam and raining down on the gunman's head. As the alien detected the movement, it spun around and delivered a barrage of harmless laser fire. In the darkness, the ray gun cast a flickering red glow over everything. The searing of the laser was loud and unearthly. Mattie dove to the floor just as the gunman fired in surprise and panic at the alien. Then Mattie heard a spitting sound: the crackle of shattered electronics. Bits of plaster showered down on the back of his neck.

"Run!" Mattie shouted.

A small electrical fire had erupted from the chest of the wounded alien, and by its light Peter could see his friends sprinting from the villains, toward the stairs and catwalk. To his left, Peter saw the Jester running away. For an instant Peter felt an odd rush of pleasure that the Jester was escaping. The Jester was a clever enemy— smart and supremely logical. These thugs with the gun were something else entirely.

Another shot echoed across the room, shearing a bit of metal off a display. The Jester, sprinting several yards ahead of Peter, dodged the shrapnel, but in so doing tangled his feet together. He pitched headlong into a wire comic book rack and landed face-first on the floor. For a moment, the Jester did not move, and Peter, as he slowly approached, was afraid that the villain might have lost consciousness. Then Peter heard a moan. The Jester turned over, tried to rise, then gasped in pain and fell back to the floor.

During the fall the display rack had broken, and a piece of thick wire now jutted from the Jester's lower leg.

116 Blood spread in a circle around it. As Peter watched, the Jester hissed a breath, reached for the wire, and yanked it out. The bloodstain grew.

"Come on," said Peter. "I'll help you."

From somewhere in the dark, the gun went off again. A chunk of linoleum spit up from the floor near Peter's feet. He grabbed the Jester's hand. "Get up! Come on!" he commanded.

The Jester—who looked much smaller now that Peter was so close—rose with Peter's help, stumbled, then stood on the wounded leg. Eyes from deep within the mask stared at Peter. He felt a tugging at his hand and looked down, realizing that the Jester was pulling away. The villain ran off, limping on his injured leg, leaving Peter holding an empty glove.

In that instant all he could think about was how small the Jester's hand had been and how a tiny object had flashed bright and red when the hand was exposed.

Peter quickly ran off as well, hoping the other Misfits had made it to safety. The last thing he heard as he climbed the staircase to the catwalk was the voice of one of the thieves.

"Let them go, you maniac," the weary voice said. "We have the artwork. Just let them go."

chapter eight

Police Lieutenant Marvin Decker rubbed his eyes and reached into the pocket of his jacket. The pocket felt empty. He patted it, checked it again to make sure, then frowned as his mind ran through a series of thoughts: One, he hated being dragged out of bed at night. Two, he especially hated being dragged out of bed at night to work a robbery. And three—the kicker that *really* put him in a bad mood—he hated being dragged out of bed at night to work a robbery and remembering that he had left his little yellow tin of aspirin at home.

"You know," he said to the Misfits, "you're a nice group of kids, and I mean that from the bottom of my heart. But you gotta be *stupider* than a *horse's tail end!*"

Peter nodded humbly. "Yes, sir."

"Good," said Decker, "at least we understand that much. Look, kid, just because you and your friends lucked out before with that stolen computer chip doesn't mean you're police officers. And it sure as heck doesn't mean you're bulletproof." He glared at each of the Misfits, daring them to disagree with him.

Decker and his partner, Sam, were detectives with the Bugle Point Police Department, Robbery Division. At the moment, they were standing in Jonathon Sutter's office at the convention center. Decker was holding the report Jonathon Sutter had filed with the police department two days earlier, when the Jester stole the Hyperman film.

"I see here, Mr. Sutter," said Decker, "that you've been having some problems here at your—whatchamacal-lit—Comicon. When you reported the initial theft, the department sent uniformed officers to investigate. Tonight, because of the…added factor.…" Decker paused.

"You mean the gunshots," Byte said.

"Right. Because of the gunshots, the captain has asked my partner and me to take over the investigation. So tell me what happened. Slowly. Sam doesn't write very fast."

Sam rolled his eyes.

"Well," said Byte, "it started on Thursday, when fire-works and gas filled up the movie theater and the Jester stole the Hyperman movie."

"Jester?" Decker said. "Oh, that's right, the report did say something about a costume. You mean he was dressed like a court jester—with bells hanging from a spiky hat?"

"No," said Jake. "No—like the villain. In the comic books."

Decker gave a doubtful nod. "Uh-huh."

"I can describe him," said Mattie. "He was wearing a purple suit with yellow stripes, a purple cape with a hood, yellow gloves, and a face mask with a big red smile on it."

"Uh-huh," said Decker. "A cape. A mask. Purple stripes."

"*Yellow stripes,*" corrected Mattie.

Sam stopped writing, frowned, and looked up from his notepad. "Was this a spooky, Dracula kind of cape," he asked, "or more like a fluttery, Batman sort of thing?"

Decker didn't like what he heard. The pair of thieves, whom none of the kids could describe, was a complication to this whole Jester matter. And the only leads Decker had were an empty rubber glove, a description of a comic collector whose only suspicious action was running away from a guy—Jake—who was chasing him, and the name of an angry artist who seemed to have at least fifty alibis for the theft of the film. Decker turned off his tape recorder, signaled Sam that he was finished asking questions, then turned back to the Misfits. "Next time," he said, "call me first."

"Yes," said Sutter, "going after the Jester on your own was a very foolish thing to do. All of you might have been hurt."

A shock of hair fell across Peter's forehead. He pulled his fingers through it to get it out of his eyes. "Let me ask you this, Lieutenant," he said. "If we *had* called you, and we had told you about smoke and riddles and costumed comic book villains, would you have believed us?"

Decker had to think about that for a moment. He remembered how these kids had helped him once before, but still—this story about a Jester might have sounded too crazy.

"I like to think so, kid," he said. "I like to think so."

Decker excused the teenagers and said good night to Jonathon Sutter. It was past midnight, and they all looked exhausted. Besides, the policemen had some things to discuss. After the group disbanded, Decker and Sam headed down the hallway toward the convention center entrance. Decker waited until he and Sam were down the hall and out of earshot before he began.

"This is not going to be easy," he said. "The stolen item is a piece of artwork—well known, easily identifiable. Whoever stole it knows how to get rid of it. Probably arranged a buyer weeks ago." Decker rubbed his eyes as they trudged down the hall. "So this is what I want. Get an evidence team down into that dealer room. Tonight—*now*—before the crowds start showing up for tomorrow's events. I want every chip in the floor and every hole in the wall checked for bullet fragments. There are bound to be some in that robot alien, so check there too. We'll also check for fingerprints on the broken glass from the art frame."

"Right," said Sam. "The Jester wore gloves, but the other perps didn't."

Decker reached into his jacket pocket and pulled out a plastic evidence bag containing the Jester's lost glove. "And we have this," he said. "I'll have Weese take a look at it in the lab, see what he can come up with."

Their cars sat side by side near the empty convention center entrance. Decker pulled his key chain from his coat pocket, touched a button, and his car alarm chirped.

"You know, Marv," said Sam quietly, "there's another way this thing can go. The thieves may not even try to sell the artwork. If they're collectors, they could just stick it up on their basement wall, and it would never see the light of day."

Decker nodded. "I know. That's what I'm afraid of." He opened the car door and tossed his jacket into the back seat, sighing. "Come on," he said. "I need a burger."

Now that the questioning was over, Byte felt exhausted from all the excitement. She strode into the hotel elevator and hit the button for the third floor.

Lucky Robin, thought Byte. While Byte and her fellow Misfits were hiding in a dark convention room, running from crazed gunmen, and giving statements to grouchy police detectives, Robin had attended a fancy awards banquet and listened to Seduction of the Innocent.

She leaned back against the wall of the elevator and closed her eyes. She was grateful that, at least for the moment, something else was doing the moving for her. *Oh well,* she thought, *at least I didn't have to drive all the way home like Jake and Peter.* Jake had driven her the two blocks from the convention center to the hotel.

Byte felt a flash of uneasiness. Robin hadn't invited her to stay over two nights. She probably would not be expecting her.

Still, after the appearance of the Jester in the dealer room, the theft of Joe Sutter's art, the gunshots, and the questioning by Lieutenant Decker, Robin was way out of the loop as far as the Jester was concerned. Surely she would want to hear right away about the events of the evening. Byte thought of Adrian Bock's small frame and how it suited the Jester's costume. She thought of the way he had exploded when she asked him about Joe Sutter, about how he'd faltered before providing an alibi. Imagine—a famous comic artist, involved in such crimes! Robin would just die when she heard. Byte reached into her computer bag for the hotel's electronic key card. She was glad she had forgotten to return it.

She paused to look at Robin's room number. The lighting in the corridor was subdued, and the shadows were deeper than Byte remembered.

Byte knocked lightly, waited a moment, then slid her key card into the slot. Robin's voice answered faintly from the other side of the door.

"Byte?"

"Yeah," said Byte, "it's me. Sorry to come by so late."

"Get in here," Robin called quietly. "Hurry."

When Byte first entered the hotel room, she couldn't see anything at all. The lights were off, and Robin was lost in the shadows in a far corner. She appeared to be kneeling.

"Robin?"

"I knew you'd come. Don't turn on the light and don't make any noise. I don't want Daddy to see I'm awake."

Byte saw movement in the shadows. She heard a click, then saw a narrow pool of light form on the floor, cast by a small reading lamp Robin had placed there. Robin was sitting next to the lamp. She had rolled up one of her pajama legs, and she was holding a washcloth against the back of her calf.

The washcloth was soaked with blood.

Byte ran over to her. "Robin," she whispered, struggling not to raise her voice in alarm. "Are you okay? What happened to you?"

Robin looked up, and Byte saw the tears streaming down her friend's face. "Oh, Byte," she said, "I'm in so much trouble. You have to help me. Please."

"In trouble?" said Byte. "Why? What happened?"

Robin pointed at a suitcase lying open near the bed. Crumpled in the case were some pieces of clothing—a purple cape with a hood, a purple suit with yellow pinstripes, and a single yellow glove. And there, resting on top of the clothing, was a plastic mask bearing the grinning red lips of the Jester.

"Oh no," said Byte.

The first piece of business was tending to Robin's injury. Byte pulled the towel away to see a small puncture wound in the back of Robin's left calf.

"I cleaned it with soap and water," said Robin, "and I've been pressing this towel against it." The area around the wound looked bruised and swollen, but the bleeding appeared to have slowed.

"It wouldn't hurt to get a couple of stitches put in this," said Byte.

Robin drew in a quick breath. "But I can't go to the emergency room!"

Byte shrugged. "Well, you're probably okay, but you're going to have a scar."

"At this point, I can live with a scar," said Robin.

Byte examined the wound again. It had definitely stopped bleeding. All it really needed, she thought, was a bandage to keep it clean. More than likely, the hotel had a first-aid kit stashed somewhere.

"Let me see what I can find," said Byte.

She went downstairs and came back with a small bandage and a bottle of antiseptic. Robin flinched when Byte dropped some of the liquid on the wound.

"Ow," Robin protested. She looked up at Byte. "So…what do you think I should do now?"

"What are you planning to do?"

Robin paused, searching Byte's eyes. "I asked you first."

Byte thought a moment. "Well," she said soberly, "first

thing in the morning, I think we should call the others. We're bound to come up with something with all five of us working together—especially if we're really working together this time...." She shot Robin a look, and Robin let her gaze drop to her hurt leg.

Byte pressed on the bandage, and the adhesive held it in place. Robin pulled down her pajama leg and started to get up, but then collapsed, all her energy and her fight gone. "Do you hate me?" she asked quietly, easing onto her bed.

Byte looked at her gravely. "Not yet, but I'm working on it. Let's get some rest and talk about it tomorrow."

At precisely 9:00 A.M. on Sunday morning, the telephone in Peter's bedroom began to ring. Still half-asleep, he let his fingers search the top of his night table until they bumped against the telephone handset. Several seconds passed before the handset actually arrived at his ear.

"Hullo?" he mumbled.

A female voice spoke for a full ten seconds before Peter realized he had not understood a word she had said.

"Huh? Who is this?" he asked.

"It's *Byte*. Wake up, Peter. Robin and I need to talk to you. It's very important. Can you meet with us? *Now?*"

"Huh? Now?"

"*Sooner* than now," said Byte. "We're at the diner over by the convention center. I already called Jake and Mattie. *Hurry!*"

126 *Click.* The connection broke.

Hmmm. So Byte has a news flash. No problem. After spending most of the night thinking about the Jester, he had a pretty big news flash for her, too.

When Peter arrived, the others were waiting for him at a booth in the back of the restaurant. They had already ordered breakfast—including his. A plate of Bavarian waffles and a glass of orange juice sat at an empty place at the table.

Peter sat down, nodded at Jake and Mattie, and looked at the two girls expectantly. He waited for one of them to speak, but when Byte remained silent and Robin sullenly jabbed her fork into a plate of scrambled eggs again and again, never lifting the fork to her mouth, he decided it might be best to just wade into the conversation on his own.

"Okay," he said, leaning forward and resting his elbows on the table. "We have work to do, so let's not waste time. You didn't call us out here just for breakfast. You brought us here to tell us that Robin is the Jester."

"*What?*" cried Mattie, his mouth full of pancakes.

Robin's fork clattered to her plate. She lay her head in her hands. "I don't know how you figured it out," she said quietly, "but I guess I knew from the start you would. I left the riddle because it's the Jester's trademark—but maybe, subconsciously, I wanted you to find out."

Peter reached out and touched the third finger on Robin's right hand. "Last night, when your glove pulled off," he said, "I saw something bright and red flash for a second before you ran away." He shrugged. "It took a while, but I finally realized what it was. A BPHS class ring—a *girl's* class ring. It certainly narrowed down the list of suspects." Peter leaned back in his chair. "Now I suppose the question is, why did you do it?"

Robin sighed. "That's the question, all right," she said.

"Well, you owe us an explanation," said Peter flatly. "You brought us here, lied to us—"

"We even got shot at!" added Mattie.

Robin stared down at the table as she spoke. "I know, and I'm so sorry. I had no idea anyone else would be there." She paused. "You guys, I'm really proud of my grandfather. I know he has a lot of anger, and he's kind of given up on himself, but he has a right to be angry. Sometimes I get angry *for* him." She took a deep breath and squeezed her eyes shut. "I was just so *mad* at American Comics—you know, for what they did to him."

Peter nodded, and Jake and Mattie remained still, silent.

"Well, about three weeks ago, this guy walked up to me in the parking lot after school. He said he wanted to talk to me about my grandfather. He told me how much he had always admired Grandpa's work—he even cited specific panels from comic books Grandpa had drawn. He called Grandpa's situation a 'cultural tragedy.' Finally he said something that just wrapped me right up."

"What did he say?" asked Byte.

"He put his hand on my shoulder and said, 'Maybe, together, we can finally help him.' Oh, I made some objections at the start, but the guy seemed to have an answer for everything. Every time I asked, 'But isn't it wrong?' he reminded me about Grandpa's contribution to the industry and how much the industry owes him. I fell for it all. Every time I felt a pang of guilt, or tried to tell myself that I was doing something wrong, that guy was there to pump up my anger."

"Robin," said Jake quietly, "when you stole the film, you didn't just get revenge against American Comics and Hunter Studios. People in the lecture hall got hurt from the fireworks and from breathing all that smoke."

"I didn't *know* about the fireworks," Robin snapped. "If I had—" she paused a moment, then shook her head. "Well, I don't know what I would have done."

"Where's the film now?" asked Peter.

"I turned it over to the guy," said Robin. "He and another man have it."

Jake and Mattie exchanged a glance. "The fat guy with the ponytail?" asked Jake.

Robin nodded. "And another man."

"Is the other man Adrian Bock?" Byte asked.

"No. Bock's not involved in this," Robin said miserably. "He really is just obsessed with artists' rights. He wasn't ever part of the plan."

"Okay, then," said Peter, "that explains a lot. But what about last night's robbery?"

Robin eyed Peter defensively. "Last night," she said, "was *my* idea. Grandpa has been asking American Comics for years to return that artwork to him. They've refused. But it's *his*, Peter. It *belongs* to him. Today every artist, even the worst hack, gets his artwork returned. Grandpa deserves at least that much."

"You said you didn't think anyone else would be there. The two men didn't know what you were planning?" Jake asked.

"Not exactly. But they did know about the clue, because one of them reprimanded me for leaving it. Also, I got angry when I turned over the film and might have hinted at having my own agenda. Anyway, the two guys figured out what I was up to, didn't they? They shot at all of us, and now they have the movie *and* Grandpa's artwork."

"Wait," said Mattie, "what about the Jester's laugh? That wasn't your voice."

Robin reached into her purse and took out a small object about the size of a Walkman. "They gave me this." She rotated the volume dial on the device, then touched a button. The Jester's high-pitched, shrieking laugh floated across the table. Diners at other tables stopped talking and stared at the group.

"Maybe we can get some fingerprints off that," suggested Peter.

Robin shook her head. "Not unless they're on the inside. I've been handling it all week."

Mattie, fascinated, reached into his jacket pocket for his multi-tool. "May I?" he asked.

A moment later he'd disassembled the device, careful not to wipe off any fingerprints.

"The basic part of the unit," he announced, "is a sound chip from one of the twelve-inch Jester action figures. Here's where some miniature speakers have been added on. I think they're from a Bose Wave Radio. And this looks like the digital control system from a Walkman." He looked at the others. "The guy who built this is no dummy."

"Great," said Jake. "Now we're dealing with high-tech thugs." He turned to Robin. "Who the heck *are* these guys?"

Robin shook her head. "They must have given me fake names. When I tried to look them up in the database of people who had mailed in for convention tickets, I couldn't locate them. And except for when I turned over the film, I haven't seen them at the convention. Of course, I haven't been milling around much."

"You have no idea where they might be staying?" asked Peter.

Robin almost smiled. "I *did* know. After last night, I doubt they're still there."

"I have to know something else," said Mattie. "When you stole the artwork, how did you get the lock open on the frame?"

Robin shrugged, her face an odd mix of pride and shame. "That was easy. American Comics wanted to make sure the artwork was safe, so they arranged to leave the key to the frame inside the convention center vault. I've known the vault combination since I was nine years old."

"Wait a minute," said Peter, pointing an accusing finger at Robin. "There's something else. You set us up last night! You knew all the time 'the Jester' wasn't after the costume. You tricked us so that we'd be out of your way."

Robin shrugged. "Guilty as charged," she said. "When it became obvious that the four of you were going to insist on staking out the dealer room, I had to make sure I had a chance of getting away."

Peter leaned back in his chair and crossed his arms. He tapped his foot angrily on the floor. "Okay," he said, "there's just one other question that's been bothering me. If you were planning all this, why in the world did you invite the four of us here? Surely you knew we'd get involved. And you said earlier that when you left the clue, you subconsciously thought we might figure you out."

Robin's face turned red, and she and Byte exchanged a knowing glance. "I don't know," she said. "I guess that, in a way, I knew I was getting in over my head and might need someone's help."

She leaned back in her chair and crossed her arms exactly as Peter did. Her mouth curled into a sly smile.

"Then again, Braddock," she said, "maybe I just didn't think you were smart enough to catch me."

chapter
nine

Sunday

J oe Sutter had not bothered to look through Saturday's
mail. He breathed a sigh of annoyance now and
picked up the stack. Sutter placed the monthly satellite
bill on his desk and took a cursory glance at the remaining envelopes—names he had never heard before, return
addresses of people he had never known. As always,
Sutter threw these in the trash.

Over the sound of the TV, he heard a car engine outside, the rattle of an older car that someone had
restored. Sutter remembered it as the car Robin and her
friends had arrived in the other day. It was a red
Volkswagen, an old Beetle convertible.

He rolled his wheelchair over by the picture window
and watched as Robin and two of her friends—a tall,
thin boy with glasses and a girl wearing a long, loose-
fitting dress—stepped out of the car onto the sidewalk.
Robin talked with them a moment, then shook her
head as if she were disagreeing with something they

were saying. She left them there and walked toward the house alone. Sutter heard the front door open.

"Knock knock," she called.

"In here," said Sutter.

Robin walked into the living room. She smiled sadly and gave Sutter a hug. Today, instead of the usual quick, warm squeeze, the hug lasted for several moments.

When she finally pulled away, Sutter frowned. "You're limping."

"It's nothing," said Robin. "How are you this morning?"

"Fine, fine," he said. Sutter had slept well last night. He really did feel fine.

"What are you watching?"

Sutter gazed at the television screen and puzzled over the question. "It's…it's okay," he said. "It's…I don't remember."

Robin walked around the coffee table for the remote control and lowered the volume. A long moment passed before she began speaking. "Grandpa," she finally said, "I wanted to talk to you a minute. "I—I did something, something I probably shouldn't have done, and I need to tell you about it."

"What is it?" he asked.

Robin circled the table again on her way to Sutter's wheelchair. As she passed by the desk and noticed the discarded stack of mail in the trash can, she retrieved the half dozen or so envelopes Sutter had tossed there. She glanced through them, studying the names and the handwriting on the envelopes. "I bet these are fan letters," she said.

Sutter grunted a reply. Nothing in that stack of mail interested him.

Robin's face flushed red with anger. "Why did you throw these away?" she snapped.

"I don't know those people."

"They know *you*," Robin said, her voice shaking.

Sutter gripped one wheel of his chair and pushed against it. The motion spun him around until he was facing away from her, toward the television. He touched the remote's volume control, and the room vibrated with the sound of a helicopter and gunfire. Robin, cupping her hands over her ears, strode over to the set, then reached behind it and yanked the cord from the wall.

The room, silent now, was a very different place for Sutter. He stared at the blank TV screen, then at the walls, then at the painting of Hyperman, then at himself seated in the wheelchair. In the absence of noise, everything—even his own legs, his twisted, arthritic hands—seemed different and very wrong. He gripped the remote, trembling.

"Don't—"

"Grandpa," said Robin, "these people care about you!"

Sutter shook his head. "I'm tired," he murmured. "I'm tired, and they all want something from me."

"So *give* it to them!" Robin almost screamed at him. "What they want is the real Hyperman, the one you and Barry created. Not this new Hyperman—"

Sutter let out a weak laugh. "Who'll destroy a whole city just to beat up one bad guy?" He laughed bitterly.

"Grandpa," Robin said, "these people just want something to hold on to. Hyperman is important to them. They see him the way you do—as someone who's strong, who stands up for everything that's right." She gazed at the oil painting above the fireplace. "Remember the cover you drew for Hyperman #17? You showed me a picture of it once."

"Yes—I haven't thought of that in years," he said, his voice barely a whisper. "Hyperman had just scooped up a child from the street. He was holding the child out of danger as a car smashed into him."

Robin nodded. "Protector of the weak. That's Hyperman, Pappy," she said, her voice quivering. "That's what your fans miss."

Sutter looked at her. "You haven't called me that since you were four years old."

She knelt down in front of his wheelchair and took his hand in hers. Then she squeezed the hand and held it against her face. She remained that way, silent, and Sutter could hear her breathing become more even. Sutter's mind filled with images: Hyperman battling aliens, Hyperman sinking a U-boat, Hyperman kissing Laura Long.

"Grandpa?" Robin finally said.

"Hmmm?"

"I came by because I needed to tell you something." Her voice sounded restrained and calm, but Sutter could hear an edge to it, a tiny flicker of fear and anger.

He looked at her. "What is it?"

Robin did not answer right away. "I—I did some things," she finally said. "They were pretty stupid. I thought I was making things better, but I wasn't. It looks like I might get into some trouble."

"What? What kind of trouble?"

She looked up at him. "I'm sorry," she said. "It was just so unfair—what they did to you. I had to do something to try to change it. You're probably going to be upset with me."

Sutter stared, not comprehending. Then he remembered: the skinny boy with the glasses talking about the Jester, a theft at the comic book convention, Robin pressing him about his old contract problems. Sutter remembered the anger that had been in Robin's voice even then.

Without even realizing he was doing it, Sutter began shaking his head. "No...no...." he said, his fingers still knotted around the television remote. "I'm too tired. I'm really tired."

"Grandpa?"

She bent her head down, forcing him to look at her.

"I hate them," Sutter whispered.

"Then stop hating them. It hasn't done you any good." Robin looked at him for a moment and stood up. "My friends are going to help me try to undo some of what I've done, but I want it all to count for something, okay? I can't have you giving up on me." She wrapped her arms around his neck and kissed his cheek. "I'll see you later. Love you."

Before he could utter a word, she was gone. He heard the front door slam, and the car outside rumbled to life. Sutter let the remote control slip from his fingers and fall to the floor. The house was quieter now than he had ever remembered. For the first time in many years, he closed his eyes and listened to the silence.

The police lab scientist tapped an empty test tube against his open palm and stared at Lieutenant Decker. "This had better be important," he said. "I'm missing *Nova.*"

Decker grunted and shook his head. Marco Weese, the lab technician, was short, thin as a whippet, and wore a loose pair of black-framed eyeglasses that tended to slip off the end of his nose. Weese had cut a length of surgical tubing to use as an eyeglass strap. Now, instead of falling to the floor, the glasses would flop against his chest, and he was forever fumbling to get them back onto his face.

"Sorry," said Decker. He understood. He didn't like working on Sunday any more than the next guy did, and Weese had been working all morning. Last night the evidence team had brought in several pieces from the convention center—the robot alien, a bent wire display rack, and several bullet fragments. Decker wanted to get a lead on the thieves by this afternoon, in the hope that they had not yet had time to get rid of the stolen items. If Decker were very lucky, the thieves

138 would be both brazen and stupid, hanging around for the final day of the convention instead of packing up and disappearing.

He reached into his jacket pocket and withdrew a plastic evidence bag containing the Jester's glove. "I'd also like a fingerprint analysis on this," he said. He tossed the bag. Weese caught it, and his glasses fell off his face again.

"Latex dishwashing glove," said Weese. "Standard variety, available in any supermarket."

The forensic scientist carried the bag over to a counter, put on a set of disposable lab gloves, and used a pair of tweezer-like forceps to remove the latex glove from the bag. Next he opened a container filled with a sticky white powder, grabbed a small dusting brush, and swept a layer of the white powder across the arm and fingers of the glove. Then he held the glove up to the light and turned it over several times, studying it. Decker leaned in close to get a better look, his chin hovering over Weese's left shoulder. Weese turned and glared at him.

"You're in my light," the scientist muttered.

"Sorry," said Decker. He stepped away.

Weese turned his attention back to the glove. On its surface, just above the wrist, the powder was taking on the shape of someone's fingerprints. "There's a set here," Weese said. "Three are badly smeared, but two are clean. Right hand. Based on the angle of the prints, my guess is they belong to the kid who pulled the glove off. A teenage male, you said?"

Decker nodded.

"Let's check the inside," said Weese.

The scientist very carefully turned the glove inside out. Lots of criminals were smart enough to wipe off the exterior of a glove, Decker thought, but hopefully this one forgot that his fingers could leave prints on the inside. Weese dusted and once again held the glove up to the light.

"Bingo," he said. "Four are smeared, but the index finger looks good."

Weese photographed the print, then scanned the photo into a computer. He spent several minutes working with the software, adjusting the contrast of the print until it was pure white against a pale, blue-gray background. Decker, who knew absolutely nothing about computers other than what his six-year-old daughter taught him, got bored and poured himself some water from a dispenser.

Weese didn't turn around, but he must have heard the water burbling. "Don't come near my equipment with that," he warned.

When Weese finished the contrast adjustments, the computer began running comparisons. Inside the computer, saved on CD-ROM, was a tremendous library of fingerprints, collected from several different sources. Some the FBI had provided, some the Bugle Point PD had collected on their own. Decker watched as the computer worked, matching section after section of the fingerprint to those in its library.

Some time later the computer beeped, and the words "no match found" flashed on the screen. Marco Weese clucked and reached for the glove again. He turned it over in his hands, tugging gently here and there as he examined it thoroughly.

"Lieutenant," he said, "look at this."

He held the glove up so Decker could see it. At the base of the third finger was a tiny hole.

"Is it torn?" asked Decker.

"Look more closely," said the scientist. "See the shape—like a star? And look at these lines pressed into the rubber around the hole. Something of *this* shape, on *this* finger, stretched the rubber and almost punched through the glove…*from the inside.*"

"Probably a ring," said Decker. "With a fairly large, faceted stone."

Weese nodded. "Now look at this."

He walked Decker over to the wire display rack. One of the rack's lower hooks lay bent at an odd angle from the others, and the rack itself was twisted slightly out of shape. "Your witnesses reported that the Jester fell on this rack and injured a leg. From the way it's bent, and from the blood we found on the floor at the convention center, it was no minor scratch."

"Okay," said Decker, "so put it all together for me."

Weese shrugged. "With that kind of ring? I'll bet you your next burger, Lieutenant, that the Jester is female. And she's limping."

Peter sat in the concession area and stared, unseeing, across the dealer room. With his index finger, he slowly traced circular patterns on the tabletop as though playing a child's connect-the-dots game. The picture refused to take shape, however, and the answers to his questions eluded him. Where would these men go? What would they do with the film? Peter tapped his finger on the table, his fingernail ticking on the Formica and sounding strangely like the second hand of an old clock.

"Earth to Peter," said a voice.

Peter turned and found his friends staring at him. Robin was the one who had spoken. "Hey," she said, "are you still with us?"

Peter took off his glasses and rubbed his eyes. "Sorry. I've been thinking. These guys have a 70mm copy of the Hyperman movie. I figure there's only one thing they can do with it."

"Make copies and sell it," suggested Jake.

"Good luck," said Mattie. "How many people do you know who own a 70mm movie projector?"

"Right. As reels of 70mm film, the Hyperman movie is worth nothing," Peter agreed. "Without the right equipment, no one can watch the movie. To make any money, these guys are going to have to find a way to convert the film to video."

"Okay, okay," said Byte, "but *how* do they do that? What's the process for converting a reel of film to video? They could just run the film and aim a video camera at the screen, but that would make a pretty lousy copy. Then they'd have to make second generation copies from that. The final product probably wouldn't be worth watching."

"Byte's right," said Mattie. "They'll do something else. There's got to be a machine of some kind that converts film to video. They run the movie through once, make a master video, then make high-speed copies off of that."

Peter leaned in close to his friends. "Right. But where do you find this machine? Ever seen one at an electronics store?"

The others shook their heads.

"Me neither," said Peter. "It's a piece of industrial equipment, probably really expensive. You'd have to find some place where they do this kind of work all the time, a place where it's someone's *job* to convert film to video. Now we have to ask ourselves, who would have a piece of equipment like that?"

"Hey," said Byte, "what about those companies that advertise that they can take old home movies and convert them to video? Doesn't that sound like what we're looking for?"

Mattie shook his head. "Nope. Old home movies are in 8mm or Super 8mm. The Hyperman film is 70 mm."

"So what's the difference?" asked Jake.

"Look at it this way," explained Mattie. "The equipment those guys use is like Peter's Volkswagen. What we're looking for is more like a Mack truck."

Robin's face brightened. "Hunter Brothers Studios," she whispered.

"That's what I was thinking," said Mattie.

"I bet the guy with the ponytail is the one connected with Hunter Brothers," Robin said slowly. "One time he got really mad at his partner, and he started shouting something about the film and how we wouldn't be able to do anything with it without his 'talents.' I didn't realize until now what he meant."

Byte turned to Robin. "There's another question, too," she said. "How far do we want to go with all of this?"

Good point, Peter thought. If the Misfits found and caught these thieves, it was a dead certainty that Robin's involvement would become known. She had made a mistake, but how much should she have to suffer for it? If the Misfits did nothing and let the men go, Robin would have to answer only to her conscience. The men would disappear, they would get away with everything, and the thefts would go unsolved. The Jester would remain a mystery, a bit of fodder for late night hotel room chats at future conventions.

Peter turned to Robin and waited.

"Hey," she said, "I messed up big time. My intentions were good, but my judgment was lousy. Don't worry about me. I'll take whatever punishment is coming. If I cooperate with the police, how bad could it be?" She looked at Peter. "Don't answer that."

"If we can find these guys before the police do," said Peter, "it might go a long way toward getting you out of trouble. We'd better get going."

144 Four members of the group rose, each tossing some money on the table to cover the meal and tip. Only one stayed seated. Mattie stared up at the others, fork in hand, a huge bite of pancakes speared on the end. "Hey," he said, "I haven't finished my breakfast...."

Jake stood over him and yanked Mattie right out of the booth. Mattie looked like a kitten dangling by the scruff of its neck.

"Your pancakes are cold," Jake said. He began walking toward the door, dragging Mattie along with him. Robin and the other Misfits followed.

As they left, Mattie's tortured voice echoed across the diner. "But—but I *like* 'em cold!"

Joe Sutter hadn't moved in the hour since Robin left. He sat in his wheelchair in the living room, the silence echoing around him.

Now his eyes fell to the table and to the mail she had left there. "The real Hyperman," he muttered, "the one Barry and I created." Sutter looked at one of the envelopes. The address was written in a child's hand-writing—scrawled, block letters. His hand shook as he slowly slit open the envelope.

> *Dear Mr. Sutter,*
> *My name is Billy. I am 9 years old. Hyperman is my favorite comic book hero. I like the old Hyperman from a long time ago better than the new one. One*

day when I was sick and stayed home from school, my daddy brought home an 80 page GIANT Hyperman. The stories in it were real old, like when Hyperman was exposed to radioactive blue mycronite and turned into a giant bug. At first I thought it was weird, but then I liked it a lot. I liked it especially when Starblaster brought another sun real close to Earth and tried to burn Earth up, and Hyperman just blew the sun out with his hyper breath.

My daddy says you're real famous and that you might get so much mail that you can't write back to me or do me a sketch. That's okay. I just wanted you to know that I like Hyperman a whole lot. When I'm bigger, I'm going to get all the old issues, just like my 80-page GIANT Hyperman. Daddy says I'll have to wait until I have a really good job to do that.

Yours truly,
Billy

Sutter read the letter a second time, and then a third. When he finished the third reading he began to laugh.

He quickly spun his chair around, and the metal bar he used for turning made his palm tingle. He looked at the red mark on his palm, staring at his hand for a long moment.

This hand, and the mind that controls it, had created Hyperman. American Comics had not. Hunter Communications had not. Joe Sutter and his best friend had

146 done it all. Sutter had held the brushes that made the pictures come to life. His partner, Barry Nagel, had given Hyperman words to speak and adventures to live. Hyperman had always been a work of the heart for the two men. And *that* Hyperman, the Hyperman that belonged to him and to Barry and to no one else, should not die. Robin was right.

He pressed his palms against the plastic armrests on either side of the wheelchair, touched his slippered feet to the floor, and slowly pushed himself to his feet. The muscles in his legs were weak from lack of use, and they quivered as he rose.

He stood, studying his hands. He clasped them together, interlocked the fingers as best he could, then stretched. The fingers crackled. There was pain, but it was bearable. Sutter stretched them a second time. They crackled again, but with less pain this time. When he held them up, they seemed a little straighter.

Maybe, he told himself, *hate twisted up your insides so much it made some of your outsides twisted, too. Let go of the hate, and everything will look straighter.*

His fingers weren't hurting so much now. He picked up the phone and called his son to ask if he had time to run him by the art supply store. Before leaving the office to pick him up, Jonathon Sutter—in disbelief—asked his dad to repeat the request three times.

An hour later Sutter shuffled over to his drafting table and pulled off the cover. It was time to get to work. He took a brand-new sheet of eleven-by-seventeen-inch art board, clipped it to the table so it wouldn't slide around, then sharpened a blue pencil. For the first time in almost two decades, Joe Sutter began to draw.

It would be a simple sketch, perhaps nothing more than a head shot of the character. Just the face, the swirling spit-curl in the hair, a bit of the cape, a hint of the chest emblem. He would ink the sketch with real india ink and brushes—*not* a marker!—and he might even throw down a few strokes of watercolor. Billy would be pleased.

The pencil sketch took half an hour. The inking occupied most of the afternoon. In his prime, Sutter could have finished the entire painting in ninety minutes, but this was just his first attempt. It wasn't bad, and he'd get faster with practice.

When he finished, he sat down at his desk and took out a sheet of paper.

Dear Billy, he wrote, *Thank you for your letter. I'm flattered that you like my work so much. By the way, let me tell you how hard it was to draw all of Starblaster's tentacles....*

chapter
ten

Charles Leach sat in the passenger seat of Wilson Dominic's car, his right hand braced against the dashboard as the car careened along a winding road. Dominic's idea of saving time was to avoid the curves by driving in as straight a line as possible, even if that path occasionally took him into a lane of oncoming traffic.

Dominic's car was an ancient Pinto, and Charles doubted that it even met the safety requirements of a bicycle. It looked like a Dalmatian—white, but with dark spots all over it where the paint had worn and the steel frame had rusted through. And the Pinto rode like a two-seater airplane in a tornado: it seemed to be expending as much energy bouncing up and down as it did going forward. The vehicle was so embarrassing to be seen in—and could potentially attract so much attention—that Charles tilted his head down at every stoplight, hunched his shoulders, and shaded his face with his hands.

For the last several months, the plan had belonged to Charles. He had thought of it, had orchestrated it, had recruited its participants. And in his opinion, he could not have done a better job of carrying it out. Now, though, he was reaching the part of the plan he most dreaded. Yes, it had been easy for him to joke, easy for him to call Dominic a caveman, easy for him to question why he had involved the brute at all. But the truth was, Dominic's technical skills had contributed to the plan's success. Charles had thought of the Jester's electronic laugh box, but Dominic had created it. Dominic had acquired the parts and made the thing *work*. Charles would not have known where or how to begin such a project.

Now Dominic's skills would become the key to the plan's fruition. Only Dominic, with the help of the equipment at Hunter Brothers Studios, could convert the 70mm Hyperman film into a high-quality video master. As a technician in the studio's video transfer lab, Wilson A. Dominic spent most of his working hours converting film to video and flipping through *Wizard* magazine. Perhaps only three or four dozen people in the entire country could operate this equipment, and Dominic, with his desperate hunger for comic book collectibles, was easy to manipulate.

Charles nervously chewed his lower lip. He could see in the young man's leer that Dominic was relishing his new role. Dominic, like the Sutter girl, was growing more independent of Charles, more convinced of his own importance.

"Don't you think we could slow down a bit?" Charles asked, shouting over the engine clatter.

Dominic said nothing, but Charles was sure he saw the young man smirk. The needle on the speedometer crept upward.

Two stone pillars announced the entrance to the studio. Between the pillars stood a wrought iron arch, an iron gate, and a uniformed security guard in a small guardhouse. Dominic screeched the Pinto up to the entrance and pulled a photo ID badge from the glove box. The guard made him sign a sheet because Charles was with him, and Charles, keeping his head down, used a phony name to sign on as a visitor. The Pinto's tires squealed and threw up dust as Dominic pulled away.

"Told you it'd be easy," he said.

Charles chose not to respond. "Where's the lab?"

Dominic pointed. "There."

"Will anyone else see us?" asked Charles.

"Don't worry. On Sundays there's usually only one person working."

"And who's scheduled to work today?"

Dominic smirked. "I am."

The lab itself was in a small stucco building. The first thing Charles noticed was how much bigger the lab looked from the inside than it did from the outside. Charles had expected the lab to be cavelike—small, poorly lit, a dark hole where warlocks like Dominic spent their days working high-tech magic spells. He could not have been more wrong. Fluorescent lights along the length of the ceiling gave the room the shockingly bright look of a mall store. Several computer stations lined one wall, each station connected to a black metal box that appeared to be some kind of special VCR. Charles felt at home in this clean, almost sterile place.

"Here's my baby," said Dominic.

When he touched a switch, lights flickered and a machine began to hum. Dominic ran his fingers over some switches. At seven feet tall and more than five feet across, the machine looked as if a person could spend years figuring out how it worked.

"It's a Telecine machine," said Dominic.

Charles whistled. "And what, precisely, does a...Tel-e-cin-e machine do?"

Dominic unzipped a bag and removed the large metallic disk containing the first reel of the Hyperman movie. "Exactly what we want it to do," he said. "It converts film to video."

In his too-tight T-shirt and jeans, and with his oversized belly and scraggly hair, Dominic looked more like an unkempt tourist than a technician. But he certainly seemed at home in the computer lab. He loaded the reel onto the machine, turned on one of the computers, and sank into a chair. The film rolled, and Charles saw the movie playing on the computer screen.

"What's wrong with it? It looks funny," he said.

Dominic nodded. "Right. Film and video are different media. When you convert one to the other, the color gets all wacko. What we normally do is run the film through one reel at a time and color-correct each scene as we go."

Charles frowned. "But there could be hundreds of scenes in an action movie," he said. "How long does this take?"

"Sometimes weeks," said Dominic.

"*What?*"

Dominic laughed and began keying commands into the computer. "Not to worry," he said. "We're taking a shortcut."

Charles watched the computer monitor, and the picture began changing. The movie became brighter, the colors more vibrant.

"I'm going to 'one-light' it," Dominic said.

"Hmmm?"

Dominic growled with impatience. "I'm going to use one set of correction commands for the whole film. It won't be perfect, but all the little fanboys out there won't care. Trust me, Chuck."

Charles stiffened at the use of the nickname. Dominic was quickly becoming too big for his size fifty-two trousers. But dealing with Dominic would have to wait. Charles still needed him for a time. Charles had long ago arranged for a distributor for his little video enterprise, who, in turn, had placed advertisements on the World Wide Web and in several small fanzines. Orders for the video were no doubt piling up at the anonymous e-mail address. The distributor had already ordered ten thousand copies. Ten thousand videos at twenty dollars apiece equaled two hundred thousand dollars.

For that kind of money, Charles could tolerate Wilson Dominic a little longer.

"Wait," said Robin, "is that them?"

She pointed as a creaky-looking Ford Pinto stopped at the studio entrance. Robin and the Misfits, packed into every square inch of Jake's Escort, craned their heads and watched as the Pinto squealed onto the studio lot.

"It's worth checking," said Peter.

Jake had parallel parked along the street, perhaps a hundred yards from the studio entrance. For the last couple of hours the Misfits had sat here, watching the studio entrance.

Peter frowned. "Getting in there isn't going to be easy," he said.

The Pinto had flown past the gate with only a moment's hesitation. Peter, however, did not delude himself into thinking that he and his friends, without any sort of authorization, would get through as easily. "We need to get past the guard," he said. "One of us will have to get in without being seen, scope the place out, and then find a way to let the rest of us in."

After a few moments of silence, Jake began watching Mattie, who was occupying himself by tugging the removable cassette player from the dashboard of Jake's car. A moment later, Byte, Peter, and Robin began gazing steadily at Mattie as well. The four watched him, waiting.

"So what are we going to do?" Mattie asked, examining the stereo's inner workings. He glanced up at his friends, his eyes flickering doubtfully from one Misfit to another. "Hey," he said, "what's everyone looking at me for?"

Peter grinned. "Mattie, I have a plan."

Roland P. Graves thought that being a security guard at Hunter Brothers Studios was better than just about any of the ten or so other jobs he had suffered through in his lifetime. His last had been at the pet store in the mall, a job he had almost liked until the day he accidentally let the ferrets out of their cage and had to retrieve them amid the screeches of terrified birds and the high-pitched yappings of startled puppies. Roland's life was just one long series of accidents.

But being a security guard was okay. Roland didn't even mind working on a Sunday. His girlfriend had long ago dumped him, he had nothing better to do, and Sundays paid time and a half—time and a half for stretching out his legs and catching up on the Sunday funnies. Yup, this job was working out pretty darn well, if Roland did say so himself.

He heard footsteps coming toward him and had to look up from his newspaper. What was this all about? Four teenagers—two boys and two girls—were walking toward the guard house. Roland sighed and got up from his chair.

"Is there something I can help you kids with?" he asked. He let one hand rest on the can of pepper spray at his belt, just to let these punks know he wasn't fooling around.

A skinny guy with dark hair and glasses stepped forward. "Yes, I hope so," he said, "Mr. ahhh…" he stared at Roland's name badge, "…Graves. Yes, Mr. Graves, it's a pleasure to meet you. My friends and I are visiting in town, and we thought we'd come by Hunter Brothers Studios, because we want to meet Pamela Anderson."

"Huh?" said Roland.

"You know," said the kid with the glasses, winking at him. "Pamela Anderson. Also known as Pamela Anderson Lee—she *was* married to Tommy Lee, but they're divorced. She's the girl from *Baywatch*. The blond one, you know?"

Roland stared at the guy blankly.

"Are you from Jupiter or something?" asked the guy. "I'm talking about *Baywatch*—the most popular TV show in the whole world, okay? I don't know why it hasn't won an Emmy. We're real big fans of Pamela's. I even wrote her a letter once, but it must have gotten lost in the mail because I never heard back. We heard she was shooting a movie out here, and we thought we'd come by to meet her."

Then a really big guy spoke. "Yeah," he said, "we want to meet Pamela Henderson."

"Anderson," said the first kid.

"Yeah, Anderson. Er…Lee."

The first guy pointed over Roland's left shoulder. "Hey, is that David Hasselhoff?"

Roland turned to look, but didn't see anyone except old Mr. Ingersoll, the weekend custodian. He turned back to glare at the teenagers. "Look," he said, "there's no filming going on today, all right? Pamela whatserface ain't here. And even if she was, which she ain't, I couldn't let you in. All right?"

The kid with glasses frowned. "That's strange," he said. "We called ahead and everything. Someone from the film crew was supposed to meet us here at the gate."

A girl with curly red hair was tapping her feet and glaring at the kid with glasses. "What*everrr*," she said. "I told you they wouldn't let you in. Can we go home now?" Then she looked at Roland. "It's like he's fixated on her or something, you know?"

"I am not," said the kid with glasses.

"He *is*," said the girl. "He watches her shows, he sees her movies, he buys her posters. It's like he idolizes her or something. You'd think I'd be enough for him, but *noooo*. He even bought the calendar. Can you believe that? $17.95 for a Pamela Anderson calendar? Plus tax! For $17.95, he could have taken me to a movie or dinner or something, don't you think?"

Roland shrugged. "Hey, leave me out of it, okay?"

"I *need* a calendar," said the kid with glasses.

"Yeah," said the big kid, "he *needs* a calendar."

"Oh? And who asked you?" said the girl. She turned to Roland. "See what I have to put up with? I should just break up with him, don't you think?" She paused then and eyed Roland's uniform admiringly. "Hey," she said, "what time do you get off for lunch, anyway?"

"Huh?" said Roland.

Finally the fourth member of the group stepped forward, a small girl with long hair and glasses. Adjusting the strap on the black nylon bag hanging from her shoulder, she looked at Roland and smiled sympathetically. "Don't worry about it," she said. "They're like this all the time." She took the other girl by the arm and dragged her away from the gate. The two guys followed.

Roland shook his head. He sat back down in his chair, glanced at *Garfield,* and looked quickly over his shoulder—just in case. He didn't want to miss a glimpse of Pamela Anderson.

Roland heard a sound from the studio lot behind him, shoes crunching on gravel, and he turned around to see another teenager walking toward him. Roland didn't remember signing him in, but more than one large group had come in this morning to set up the shoots for the week. Roland might have forgotten a face. Surely if the kid was on the lot, he must *belong* on the lot. Must be a grip or something—or maybe some kid hired at minimum wage to do all the little jobs the big shots didn't have time for.

The kid, who was barely five feet tall, didn't act like a grip. He walked up to the gate as if he owned the entire

158 studio. "Morning, Roland," he said, and he gave the guard a friendly clap on the shoulder. "Excuse me." He stepped up to the gate and began waving at the four teenagers who were heading back to their car. "Hey," he called, "sorry I'm late. You the Braddock party? Here to meet Pamela Anderson?"

The four teenagers walked back toward the gate. They stepped onto the studio lot, signed in on Roland's clipboard, and waved at him as they passed.

"It's okay," said the kid. "They're with me." From a distance, he quickly flashed an ID with his photo on it.

Roland looked at the kid. He sure seemed young to be working at the studio. Something wasn't right. His eyes narrowed, and his hand dropped once again to the leather holster containing his can of pepper spray. "Hey," he said, "what division do you work in?"

The kid's eyes fluttered for a second, then he smiled. "I'm in stellar cartography," he said. He turned to join the others, and the group of them wandered off onto the lot.

Roland stared at the teenagers, shook his head, then returned his attention to his Sunday paper. He didn't know what they did in stellar cartography, but it sounded pretty technical. That kid must be a genius or something.

Once they were a safe distance from the guard shack, Mattie showed his "studio ID" to the others. It was a BPHS student body card. "How'd I do?" he asked.

Jake wrapped a thick arm around Mattie's neck and gave the younger boy's head a knuckle rub. "You did great, stellar cartographer," he said. "You've just seen too many *Star Trek* movies."

Peter looked over the studio lot. He had known that it would be big, but he hadn't been prepared for anything of this scale. The lot was immense, probably several square miles. He frowned. "We'll have to split up," he said. "We're looking for a building with a name like 'Video Processing Lab' or 'Video Transfer,' okay?"

They threw together a quick plan. Peter, Byte, and Robin would try one direction; Jake and Mattie would try the other. They would meet at the gate in an hour. At that time, if they had found anything, they would call Lieutenant Decker. "Okay, then," said Peter. "Let's get going."

Mattie and Jake trudged off toward the west side of the lot. Peter stared at a cluster of identical buildings in the distance: small, beige stucco boxes that blended with each other and with the sand and gravel.

"This could take all day," he said.

Robin tapped him on the shoulder. "Or not," she replied. "Look." She pointed at a building slightly larger than the others. "See the red Miata?" she asked. "Now look just past it. Isn't that our clunker?"

Peter nodded. "Stay behind me," he said.

The two girls looked at each other and rolled their eyes.

As they crept toward the building, Peter grew more hesitant. He did not like this approach at all—daylight, a windowed building, no cover. Anyone inside the video transfer lab needed only to glance through a window, and Peter and the girls would be seen.

"We can't let anyone know we're here," he said. He motioned to the corner of the building. "Let's head around to the back."

They lowered their heads, moved around the building, and slid into position beneath a window. From here, the three of them rose slowly and peered inside.

"We've got 'em," whispered Robin.

Two men were in the lab. One was the guy Peter had seen in the lecture hall. His filthy ponytail was unforgettable. He was staring at a computer screen, his back to Peter. A man with a slick haircut, no doubt the one who had recruited Robin, paced around the room.

The pacing man was talking incessantly, moving about the room, throwing nervous glances at the door. Peter couldn't read his lips, but he quickly understood something: *This is not the man to fear. The dangerous man is the one at the computer station.* The ponytailed guy turned slightly to say something. In the bright light of the monitor screen, his round face had taken on a hard, malevolent look, a look Peter hadn't noticed at the Comicon. His posture at the computer—shoulders hunched, head bowed—seemed focused and assured rather than weak.

"What are they doing?" asked Robin.

"The film is over there," whispered Byte. "On that machine. See it? And that slot there looks like it's for a blank videotape. I'm not sure what the computer is for, though. Maybe it controls the machine, or maybe they're using it to make some kind of corrections as they convert it."

Peter and Robin ducked down but Byte remained at the window, studying the equipment inside the lab.

"Okay," whispered Peter. "We've seen enough. Let's find the others and call Decker."

Robin shook her head. "Braddock," she said, "if they finish making the video before the police get here, they'll leave. We need to figure out a way to keep them here without actually letting them finish."

"And without getting shot," added Peter.

"Yes, that would be nice too."

Byte was still peering through the window at the computer screen, straining to see how the ponytailed guy was working the keyboard. "Okay," she finally said. "I think I can slow these guys down and keep them here a while longer. I'm not sure how much time it will give us, but I have an idea." She crept away from the building.

"Hey," whispered Peter, "where are you going?"

"I'm not sure," said Byte, "but if my idea works, you'll be the first to know."

She disappeared around the corner.

Robin took another look through the window, then spun away and sat down hard in the dirt. She squeezed her eyes shut and muttered, "Stupid, stupid, stupid!"

"What happened?" asked Peter.

"The guy at the computer looked up and started talking to his friend," Robin moaned. "I ducked as fast as I could."

"Did he see you?"

Her body trembled a bit as she spoke. "I don't think so," she said. "I hope not."

Dominic rose from his chair and walked over to a shelf by the main door. On the shelf were several bottles, chemicals for cleaning or maintaining the equipment. He reached for one of the bottles and poured its contents into two white cleaning rags, saturating them. The strong odor that wafted through the room made the inside of Charles's nose tingle.

"Is there a problem?" asked Charles.

Dominic looked at him with a wicked grin. Perhaps it was the fluorescent lights in the ceiling, but Dominic's eyes gleamed savagely with a wildness Charles had not seen there before.

"Nah," whined Dominic. "No problem." He was still smiling when he quietly opened a side door.

"One of them is leaving," said Robin.

Peter peeked through the window. He could just see a door closing. "What does that door lead to?" he asked.

Robin shrugged. "Don't know. Maybe it's a storage room or something. Maybe he's getting another piece of equipment."

Peter nodded, turning his attention again to the window. Perhaps Robin was right. The guy with the ponytail had probably just gone to get a tool, or a computer manual he needed.

Just then Peter heard the crunching of gravel behind him, pebbles crushed beneath a heavy boot. A thick arm wrapped around Peter's neck, and a wet cloth clamped over his mouth and nose. He struggled to see Robin. The attacker's other arm held a cloth over her face as well, covering everything but her wide, pleading eyes. A chemical smell seared the inside of Peter's nostrils, drying out his nasal passages, moving further and further into his head. The smell grew like a cloud, filling his mind until there was nothing else at all—no lab, no studio, no men, no Robin—and everything went cold and black.

b yte trudged across the sand and gravel, looking for an unlocked office. One of the squat, boxy-looking buildings lay just ahead, and Byte could see that someone was inside. She walked up to the door, feeling a flash of nervousness as she reached for the doorknob. She counted to herself, three seconds for extra courage, then opened the door without knocking.

The room was a large office. Partitions set off several cubicles, and a young woman sat working at one of the desks. She wore an enormous pair of glasses with perfectly round frames. At the sound of the door opening, she leaned back and watched Byte enter. "Hi," she said. "Can I help you?"

"I just need to use a phone," said Byte. "Is that okay?"

The woman shrugged and pointed toward a row of unoccupied desks.

Byte chose the farthest cubicle and sat, thinking. The electronic line leading to the video lab would be a secure number, so it would not likely appear on a regular phone list. She opened the Rolodex file on the desk, flipped through the *V*s, but found no listing. Next, she began quietly rifling the desk drawers, looking for a laminated sheet or a card. She found nothing.

If I worked here, she asked herself, *where would I—*?

She thought a moment, then reached for the Rolodex and turned it over. There, taped to the bottom with transparent tape that had yellowed over time, was a plastic card listing a series of phone numbers leading to the studio's various computer systems. At the bottom of the list was Video Transfer Laboratory.

Byte plugged the phone cord into her modem jack and opened her computer. She typed in the phone number, keyed in a few commands, and in moments she was tied into the computer system in the video lab. Two or three false starts—attempts to connect to wrong areas of the system—slowed her down, but she eventually patched into Dominic's computer. *This has got to be it,* she told herself. There, streaking across her computer screen, was Hyperman. He flew up the side of a building, catching a falling helicopter with one hand and rescuing his girl-friend, reporter Laura Long, with the other.

Hmmm, thought Byte, *cool special effects.*

She frowned at the menu list at the top of the screen. The color-correction software was more complicated than she had imagined, and she wasn't quite sure how to proceed. Then again, she supposed, it didn't really matter what she did or how she did it.

Her finger hovered over one of the function keys. *Let's see what happens, she thought, if I do this....*

Peter's sinuses still burned, and his vision was blurred. Several moments passed before he could see clearly enough to know that he was inside the video lab. He could tell that Robin was seated behind him, her back to his. He could feel her struggling. Byte was missing— either caught somewhere, or free to find the others.

He tried to rise, but couldn't. His shoulders ached because his arms were pulled tightly behind him, bound with duct tape and fastened to the back of his chair. Tape bound his ankles as well, securing them to the chair's legs.

His captors stood near a row of computer terminals lining the wall. They whispered angrily at each other, occasionally glancing in Peter's direction.

"*Are you crazy?*" hissed the guy with the slick haircut. His face was red. "We planned a simple theft. That was all!" He pointed at Peter. "I never planned for hostages."

The man with the ponytail sneered. "You didn't plan for *anything*," he said. "These brats have been after us the whole time. Can't you see that? And the Sutter girl even helped them! Did you want me to just sit here and let them spy on us? Maybe you'd like me to hand her the phone so she can call the police and turn us in!"

The first man's mouth quivered, but he stood a little straighter, fortifying himself against the other's attack.

"Don't forget, I am in charge here," he said. "What I say goes."

The man with the scraggly ponytail said nothing. He walked over to a chair, grabbed a gym bag, and reached inside. When he withdrew his hand, something glinted in the light.

It was a gun.

"I'm sick of this," the ponytailed man said. His breathing was uneven, and his forehead glistened. "Even at the beginning, you treated me like I was nothing. Like I was *stupid.*" His eyes looked wild and unseeing.

"Funny thing is," he continued, "you *always* needed me. You promised me a full share of the profits for helping you, because you couldn't pull this off by yourself. I'm not about to let the plan change now. This gun says *I'm* in charge."

The first man swallowed, and when he spoke again he practically whimpered. "Well, you can't kill them. It's crazy. Even if they have seen us...."

The other man said nothing. He just went back to the bag and drew out a second gun. "Nah," he said, "I won't kill them. I'm just going to stop them from following us when we're finished."

He set a pair of clamps on opposite sides of the room and placed a gun in each clamp. He adjusted the height of the clamps, eyeing down the sight of each gun as he did, and Peter soon realized that one of the weapons was pointed at him, the other at Robin. The man then tied a length of twine to the trigger of each gun, threaded the

168 twine through the light fixtures in the ceiling, and tied the other ends to Peter's and Robin's wrists. Peter caught a nauseating whiff of chemicals on the man's hands. When the man finished, he cocked the hammer back on each gun.

"Pretty smart, huh?" he said to Peter. "If you move your wrists, the gun behind you goes off and kills the girl. And if the girl moves—boom!—*you* get it." He grinned, altering his voice to the modulated cadences of a television announcer. "Will the Dynamic Duo be turned into the *dead* duo?" he asked. "Tune in tomorrow—same bat time, same bat channel!"

The first man gazed at the computer screen and squinted. "Hey," he said, "something's wrong here. The picture's getting too dark."

"Huh?"

His partner ran back to the computer and began tapping the keys. He cursed and typed some more, and the picture on the screen grew brighter. "There," he said, "I've corrected it. Everything's fine."

Darn, thought Byte. *They fixed that problem.* She studied the file names again. Most of them didn't make any sense to her, but then, they didn't have to, did they? She scrunched up her nose to keep her glasses from falling and keyed in another command.

The first man wiped a sleeve across his forehead. "Now it's turning all green!" he said. "Why is it doing that?"

The other man tapped in more commands, but Hyperman turned even greener. The guy slapped his palm against the side of the computer. "I don't know!" he shouted. "This hasn't ever happened before! Maybe the film itself is messed up."

Sweat ran in glistening lines down his face. His eyes narrowed, and he turned toward Peter. "It's you, isn't it?" he said. "Somehow you and your friends are doing this." His tone was low and even, but a tiny muscle began twitching at the corner of his eye.

Then, with no warning, the man let out a bellow and launched himself at Peter. His fingers gripped Peter's hair and tightened to a fist. "*Make it stop!*" the man shouted. "*Do you hear me? Make it stop!*" Peter gritted his teeth against the pain and concentrated on keeping his hands steady.

Just then the partner intervened, grabbing the enormous man around the middle and dragging him away from Peter. The two staggered, for the smaller man was slim and could not really handle the big man's weight. Both men fell to the floor. "Dominic," the man shouted, "stop! That's *enough*. Leave the kid alone."

Dominic, thought Peter.

"Forget these kids," the man went on, panting. "We can't spend the whole day dealing with this." His voice was low and sure. "Look. Let's forget the film. It's a loss. We still have Sutter's artwork. I can get seventy-five thousand for each of us. Cash. And no one, not even the girl, knows who we are or where we'll be." The man's voice softened, became almost pleading. "If someone gets hurt, the police will never stop hunting us. Let it go. Seventy-five thousand each. It's enough. Let's just get out of here."

Dominic glared, studying his partner. "All right," he finally said. He lowered his head, and long strings of hair shadowed his face. "All right. But while we're in this, you treat me with *respect*, understand? I'm an *equal*." He turned to Robin. "And you," he said. "Remember you're in this as deeply as we are. Identify us to the police—say *anything* to the police—and we'll take you down with us."

Dominic's partner rose and offered Dominic his hand. "Let's move," he said. "Their friends are out there. Let's get out of here before we have to deal with them, too."

The men did not shut off the Telecine machine or bother taking the film with them. Indeed, they nearly stumbled over each other running out the door, and Dominic brushed against the shelf of chemicals on his way out. Two bottles clattered against each other and broke. The chemicals streaked down the wall, turning it a muddy amber color.

The door closed, and Peter heard the lock click into place. He and Robin were alone.

"Are you okay?" asked Robin.

"Yeah," said Peter. "You?"

The back of Robin's head moved against his. She was looking at the ceiling. "You know, I can't believe this," she said. "I think I saw this very same deathtrap on a rerun of the old Batman TV show."

"How did Batman get out of it?" asked Peter.

"Um," said Robin, thinking, "I think he used his Bat Gun-Deactivator or something."

"Terrific," Peter muttered. "Just terrific."

Outside, the Pinto rumbled to life, its tires scrabbling against the gravel.

The chemical mixture running down the wall reached an electrical outlet near the floor. A tiny shower of red and gold sparks burst forth, and then, almost instantly, a flame *whooshed* up the wall. The column of fire crackled and spread.

"Robin?" said Peter.

"Yeah?"

"We need to get out of here. Right now."

"What am I missing?" asked Robin. "What's that smell? What's that noise?"

"You don't want to know."

Peter's mind raced. Several feet in front of him, the gun remained in its clamp, silent and watchful, its barrel pointed at the space above his nose. The length of twine connecting his hands to the other gun trembled and grew taut with any movement he made. "Okay," he said, "let's review here. The guns are loaded and cocked."

"Right," said Robin. "And would you mind keeping still, please? I'm the one who pays if you get clumsy."

"If we yank the twine hard, the guns will go off," said Peter, thinking aloud. "But they'll only fire *once*."

"Braddock," Robin pointed out, "once is enough."

Peter looked at the floor, at the chair, at the space around them. It just might work. "I think we should dive for it," he said.

He could hear Robin swallowing before she replied. "What?"

"On the count of three," said Peter, "dive for the floor—to my right and your left. We plant our feet, and on three we *move*—we take the chairs down with us and everything."

"But the guns will go off!"

Peter knew that. "But they'll miss, because we'll be moving toward the floor," he said. "It'll be close, but they'll miss."

"Oh, now *that's* reassuring," said Robin. He felt her shaking her head, then heard her take a deep breath. "Okay. Are we going right when you say three, or are you going to add something clever like 'Go!' or 'Now!' or 'Geronimo!' or something?"

"I'll say—I'll say 'One, two, three, dive.' On the word 'dive,' we'll go for it." He clamped his eyes shut. "All right," he said. "Plant your feet and get ready to push hard. Ready?"

Robin paused. "Okay."

The fire had already spread over half the wall. Peter thought of the shelf of chemicals. When the fire reached it, taking down the shelf and shattering the bottles, the chemical fumes would be deadly. Or they might explode.

"All right," he said. "One…two…three…*dive!*"

As they moved, gunfire tore the air, and the wave from that blast rattled the windows. A whistling sound swept past Peter's ear. He heard the chairs clatter as they fell.

The side of his head felt warm, and he and Robin slumped to the floor.

Mattie crept up to a building and peered inside. It was dark and empty like all the others. The studio lot seemed to go on forever, seemingly even beyond the distant false storefronts and plywood western street. He turned toward Jake, heaved his shoulders in a tremendous shrug, and sat down in the dirt. "Well," he said, "this is way too much excitement for me."

"I'm hungry," grumbled Jake. He pulled his Superball out of his pocket and bounced it hard in front of him.

"You know," said Mattie, "it doesn't work like this in the Hardy Boys books. They have these exciting times solving all kinds of mysteries. Action, adventure— they've got it all. We're wandering around an empty studio lot on a quiet Sunday. I hope Peter and the girls are having more luck than we are."

Jake laughed. "Well, Peter already is," he said. "See how he fixed the teams so that *he* got to hang out with Byte and Robin?"

"Yeah?" Mattie said. "So what?"

Jake looked at him a moment. "He planned it so he's hanging out with the *girls.*"

Mattie frowned. "What's your point?"

Just then, a great *b-bang!* filled the air. The distant sound echoed against the buildings and reverberated several times before fading.

Mattie felt a tingling sensation in his knees. "What was that noise?" he asked quietly.

He looked at Jake, who grabbed his Superball and stared in the general area of the source of the sound. Mattie could tell that Jake was nervous, too.

"A car backfiring?" suggested Jake, already moving toward the sound.

Mattie followed, struggling to keep up. "We can hope," he said.

The boys looked at each other. "Oh, geez...." said Jake.

The two of them began to run.

Byte stared at her computer screen. The film had been running for a long time, and Hyperman was still just as green as ever. *Weird.* Her nose crinkled. Why weren't these guys correcting the color changes she had made? They certainly couldn't sell a video that looked like this.

Something wasn't right.

Byte quickly shut down her computer and plugged the phone back in. *I'd better get back to Peter and Robin,* she thought. *There might be trouble.*

Then she heard a sound that came from the direction of the video lab. Byte had heard an M-80 go off once, at a Fourth of July picnic several years ago. She remembered the way the huge, exploding firecracker had made her ears ring. The sound from the video lab was very similar to that.

She packed her computer into the bag and ran to the door. As Byte was leaving, the woman at the other desk glanced out the window at the noise.

"Hmmm," she said. "Must be filming today."

Byte hoped so.

A yellowish smoke that smelled like burning cloves filled the video lab. Peter's throat burned. He could hardly see.

"Robin!" he shouted. "Are you all right?"

"I'm okay," she replied. "Oh God, Peter, the bullet went right past our ears. It made a buzzing sound...."

Peter struggled to free himself from the chair, which now lay bent beneath him. But when he pulled away from it, his ankles and wrists were still bound together. He hopped over to a counter where blades used for editing videotape lay scattered. He had to turn his back to the counter to reach them, and he fumbled for one with his fingers. Moving quickly, he slashed the tape binding his wrists and ankles.

When he staggered through the smoke and found Robin, she was already free, rubbing at the chafed skin around her wrists. "Leave it to a guy to do things the hard way," she said, looking at the blade.

Peter ran to the door and tugged at the handle. It was securely locked.

He looked at the window and was greeted by the sight of Byte staring in from outside, screaming at him. She was right there at the window, but the fire inside was *whooshing* like a tornado. Peter couldn't hear what she was saying.

Then she started making motions with her arms as though she were swinging a baseball bat at the window.

Feeling foolish, Peter nodded and reached for a chair. It was a solid, industrial-type with swiveling steel casters—built to last. It probably weighed thirty pounds. Peter wrapped his fingers around the sides of that chair and swung it as hard as he could against the window.

The window cracked, but it didn't shatter. The chair bounced off the glass and clattered to the ground. Peter looked closely. The window had wire filaments running through it. It was safety glass, the same glass construction workers put in the narrow windows of schoolroom doors. Peter lifted the chair again and swung it once, twice, three times against the window. The glass shattered into tiny, murky splinters, but the wire filament merely caved in a little.

Peter wiped his sleeve across his eyes and looked around the room. In a few minutes, the smoke and fire would engulf the entire lab. Byte's face—eerily faceted, like a diamond—screamed at him through the broken glass.

"I think we're in trouble," he whispered.

Jake heard Byte screaming, then he saw the flames inside the lab. He sped up to full sprint. When he was perhaps five feet from the building, he leaped, angled himself so that his shoulder came forward, and threw all two hundred pounds of his weight against the door, only to bounce off and land in the dirt, pain searing through the muscles in his shoulder.

Interior sprinklers had kicked on, spraying the fire and sending a black cloud billowing through the lab. Something inside made spitting sounds, like bacon frying. An alarm sounded. Jake pulled himself to his feet and threw himself against the door again and again, until it splintered and the door frame gave way. Yellow-gray, acrid smoke poured through the open doorway. Jake sprawled on the floor of the lab, the shattered door beneath him, and he reached his hands into the cloud of smoke. He felt around, his fingers closing on someone's wrist. *Robin.* Holding his breath, he wrapped his arms around her and dragged her outside, then went back for Peter.

Moments later the three of them knelt in the dirt, far from the building, and they coughed until fresh air cleared their lungs. Peter and Robin had tears in their eyes, and not just from the smoke. Byte stood near them, biting her lip. Mattie stared blankly at the lab building.

In the distance, Roland the security guard ran toward them.

"Oh, man," said Robin, coughing horribly. "I thought we were going to die."

Peter's throat burned, and his eyes watered heavily. He was shaking a little. He wiped a spot of blood from the side of his head, where a bullet must have ever-so-slightly grazed the skin.

Robin tugged on Peter's shirt sleeve. "But look—" Peter looked up. Her face was covered with sweat and streaked with black grime, but she was smiling.

Lying at Robin's feet were the silver canisters containing the Hyperman movie. She had rescued the film while Peter was trying to break the window.

"We'll take this back to my dad's office," she said, and her smile lit up her sooty face like a bright lamp against a dark wall. "That's one down. One more to go."

Roland ran up to the building, and Jake, Mattie, and Byte began explaining the situation to him, interrupting each other and shouting about how the two men had gotten away.

Tiny tears lingered in Robin's eyes, and she began to cough again. She reached out and without even looking, she clasped Peter's hand in hers, giving his fingers a squeeze.

Between coughs, Peter looked at Byte and, for a moment, he wanted to pull his hand away.

But he didn't.

Studio security and fire department authorities questioned the Misfits for half an hour, determining, finally, to turn the matter over to the police. Local police informed the detective who was already in charge of the investigation—Lieutenant Decker.

After cleaning themselves up, the Misfits returned to the nearly empty convention center, accompanied by a uniformed police officer. They walked across the huge dealer room floor, ignoring the hundreds of shop owners who were slowly packing up their booths. Robin carried Jake's athletic equipment bag over her shoulder, and it bounced and clattered with the movement of the film canisters inside. She was planning to turn the film over to Decker and admit everything to her father. It would not be an easy confession.

Robin felt her heart thumping as she and her friends trotted up the stairs to her father's office.

"What on earth am I going to say?" she asked.

She stopped at the office door and looked back at the others. Peter's mouth formed a thin, serious line, and his lips were pale.

"It'll be okay," said Byte, smiling confidently. "You know what to do."

Robin faced toward the office, took a moment to gather her thoughts, then pushed open the door.

180   Lieutenant Decker and his partner were standing in the room. Their grim faces turned slowly in Robin's direction when she entered.

On her father's desktop, in a clear, plastic evidence bag, was the Jester's lost glove.

"Miss Sutter," said Lieutenant Decker, "we have a good deal to discuss."

Seeing her father's face frightened her the most. He had always been a very thin man, but now he looked weak, defeated. His cheeks seemed hollow, the circles under his eyes darker and more apparent. *I've learned something from these men,* his face was saying, *and I'm waiting for you to tell me that it's a lie.*

Robin did not even try to work around the truth. "Daddy," she said, her eyes brimming over with tears, "maybe you'd better call a lawyer."

chapter
twelve

byte watched the proceedings silently. Her first thought, and the one that caused her the most pain, was: *All our efforts, all the dangerous moments were for nothing.* Robin was in trouble, the real bad guys had escaped, and Robin's reason for taking up the Jester's cloak—protecting her grandfather— would matter little to the police. Byte's anger boiled up inside her.

"Miss Sutter," said the Lieutenant, "Do you know the names of the two men?"

"They gave me fake names," Robin replied somberly.

"Were either of the two men employees of Hunter Brothers Studios?"

"I couldn't say for sure," said Robin. "You should ask the security guard about that. But one of them seemed very comfortable with the video transfer machine, and they didn't have trouble getting onto the studio lot...."

Byte rose then and calmly walked over to the gym bag lying on the floor, the one containing the reels of film. She reached down for the straps, gingerly drew the bag onto her shoulder, and walked to the door without saying a word. Peter's eyes followed her. The policemen were too preoccupied to notice.

Where are you going? Peter mouthed.

Byte shook her head. She would explain later. Before anyone else noticed, she slipped through the door and shut it quietly behind her.

She moved down the stairs and into the convention hall. A long walk took her into the publishers' area, and she soon spied the American Comics booth. She walked up to a man she recognized from yesterday morning and waited patiently as he taped shut a box containing promotional buttons—probably leftovers from the box Mattie had scattered.

"Excuse me," she said, "I need to speak with Janine Cook right away."

The man glanced up at her. "Sorry," he said. "She's in a meeting in the upstairs conference room. I'm afraid she can't be interrupted. Would you like to—?"

Before he even finished, Byte clipped off a thank-you and strode away from the booth. She returned to the lobby, found the stairs, and headed up to the conference room.

Out of breath, she stopped at the door. She raised her knuckles, then let her arm drop to her side. *Well,* she thought, *if I'm going to interrupt an important meeting, I might as well not be shy about it....*

She took a deep breath and thrust open the door. Janine Cook sat across the table from a silver-haired man who looked to be in his sixties.

Byte said nothing. Before her common sense could kick in and dictate differently, she strode into the room and plunked the reels of film down on the carpet. The man glared at the intrusion. Janine Cook raised an eyebrow.

"Well, hello, Byte," said the publisher. "That was quite an entrance." She then turned to the man and offered him an introduction. "Jack," she said, "this is a new friend I've made here at the convention. Byte Salzmann." Then she looked at Byte with a mysterious smile. "Byte, this is Jack Hunter, president and CEO of Hunter Communications, the parent company of Hunter Brothers Studios."

"Oh?" Byte attempted not to reveal her surprise.

"Young lady," said the movie magnate, "those don't happen to be the missing reels of the Hyperman movie, do they?"

Byte nodded. "Yes, they do, sir," she said. "My friends and I tracked down the thieves who stole the film. They were attempting to make copies for distribution. The police are probably going to want to keep the reels for evidence for a while, but I wanted Ms. Cook to know that the movie is safe."

The man rested his elbows on the table. He said nothing.

"And there's something else," said Byte. She turned to Janine Cook. "I want to talk to you about an idea I have regarding Joe Sutter...."

Robin's voice was even, her eyes were clear, but Peter found himself watching her hands. Robin was gripping the arms of her chair and squeezing.

"So what happens to me now?" she asked.

Decker frowned doubtfully. He seemed reluctant to take a teenage girl downtown, especially when much guiltier parties were going to walk. "Well," he said, "we're working with the studio to track down the two men you've described. But right now, Miss Sutter, you need to understand that you are a suspect in a felony. You and your father will have to come downtown with us."

Peter did not like the helplessness that saturated the room. There had to be something he could do. He turned his mind back to those moments in the video transfer lab, trying to remember anything that might help determine the men's identities. Anything that might help Robin.

"Dominic," he muttered.

Decker scowled at him. "What?"

"Dominic," said Peter. "The guy converting the film was called 'Dominic.'"

Sam removed a small notepad from his shirt pocket and began riffling the pages. "Okay," he said, "was it a first or last name?"

"No way to tell," said Peter.

Decker leaned back in his chair and scratched at his bald spot. He looked at Robin's father. "Do you have a list of the people who attended the convention?"

Sutter nodded. "Yes, we have a database," he said. "The Comicon Committee uses it to establish a mailing list for next year's convention." Then he frowned. "We can run a name search, but it's a long shot. If these men bought their badges at the door instead of sending in for them, we might not have a record of it in the computer yet. We'd have to hand-check the application cards of everyone who attended the con. That's over nineteen thousand people."

Peter winced. The job was impossible. One name wasn't enough.

"But wait a minute," Peter said. "How did those guys manage to set up the fireworks in the lecture hall? That trick had to be prepared. Someone who just walked in off the street and bought a badge wouldn't have the access needed to set it up."

"They had Miss Sutter to help them," said Decker.

Robin shook her head defiantly. "No way," she said. "I did know there was going to be some distraction, but I didn't have the details. That stunt was dangerous. If I had known they were going to use fireworks, I wouldn't have gone along with any of it."

"Did you give them a key?" asked Decker.

"Absolutely not," said Robin.

Mr. Sutter turned to Peter. "So what are you saying?"

"I'm saying," said Peter, "that one or both of those guys had to have some access to the building. They might have been, I don't know, convention center employees. Or from a cleaning crew that works on the building. People with unusual access to the facilities."

186 Jonathon Sutter shook his head emphatically. "It couldn't have been an employee," he said. "We haven't hired any new people in almost a year. I trust *all* my workers."

"Okay," said Peter, "then maybe the men were volunteers or something." He looked at Mattie. "Let me see your convention guide."

Mattie reached into his back pocket and pulled out the folded magazine. Peter flipped through it to the last couple of pages, and there in the back, in the smallest print imaginable, was a lengthy thank-you to all the volunteers who had made the convention possible. Peter's eyes ran down the list until he came to the seventh entry. He jabbed the name with his finger: Wilson A. Dominic.

"There's your man," he said. "He could lie about his name to Robin, but he couldn't get a volunteer badge without showing his ID." He looked at the Lieutenant. "And he drives a beat-up Pinto."

Decker nodded. "Okay," he said. "I'll give it a try. Sam, call Hunter Brothers Studios, see if they have an employee by this name, and get an address. Then call the DMV and run a registration check on his vehicle. We're going to pay Mr. Dominic a visit."

Charles Leach had not spoken since the Pinto screeched away from the studio lot. He had heard the gunshots go off in the lab. When Dominic stopped the car at the gate, Charles had turned around, and he could just make out the yellow-red flickering in the lab's front window. *First gunshots,* he thought. *Now fire.* Nodding to the music in his tiny headphones, the security guard waved the Pinto through the gate. Charles leaned back in his seat and squeezed his eyes shut.

He had not counted on murder. This operation was to have been so simple. An easy theft, some quick promises to the Sutter girl, and it was all supposed to be over. How had things become so complicated? If only those kids hadn't interfered. Charles felt a deep pang of guilt that his plan had come to this, to the deaths of two young people, but at the same time he couldn't help hoping that the bodies would be burned beyond recognition. Let the fire destroy everything that might lead the police to him.

As it was, he had a more immediate worry. Dominic— his helper, his partner, his fellow *thief*—was out of control.

Dominic muttered to himself absently. "Gotta be complete," he said, his fingers tapping a machine-gun rhythm against the steering wheel. "The first one hundred issues—the first *two* hundred. Gotta get *every* issue. Gotta fill the holes. Then I'm *complete.*"

"Dominic," said Charles, "are you all right?"

Dominic's head whipped around suddenly, as though he had just realized Charles was there.

"Watch me," he said, grinning. "I get my powers from a yellow sun."

Charles gritted his teeth as Dominic screamed around corners toward his house. When they arrived, Charles could not have been more surprised by what he saw. Dominic lived in a Victorian house with white siding and a little picket fence surrounding a yellowed lawn. Many of the pickets had slipped off the fence and fallen to the ground.

Charles grabbed the leather folder containing Sutter's artwork and stepped out of the car. "This your folks' place?" he asked nervously.

Dominic spun around. "It's *my* place," he said. "My dad left. My mom died a couple of years ago."

"Sorry," said Charles as he followed Dominic up the walkway.

Dominic shrugged. "I got my interest in comic books from my dad. When I was sixteen, he nicknamed me 'Swamp Thing.'"

Charles remained silent. What could he possibly say to a comment like that?

Dominic led him inside the house. The first thing Charles noticed was the staleness of the air. Heavy drapes covered the closed windows.

"Wait'll you see this," Dominic said. "I think you'll be impressed."

Dominic led Leach through the living room, stepping over a tangle of electrical wires that criss-crossed the carpet like a net. The wires ran back and forth between stereo components, a DVD player, a computer system, and some metallic boxes Charles could not identify.

When they reached the den, Charles gasped.

"This is my collection," said Dominic.

The room was a cross between a museum and a discount table at a dime store. The centerpiece was a floor-to-ceiling bookcase housing Dominic's comic books. Charles stepped closer to it. Dominic had filed the comics in neat rows, organized by title and issue number. Transparent Mylar sealers protected the Golden Age books, which Dominic had placed facing outward, displaying them like paintings. The shelf exploded in color, the old paper filling the room with the musty scent of decaying pulp.

"Here are my *Star Wars* collectibles," said Dominic. "Don't step on Yoda."

The Yoda doll was full-sized, perhaps three feet tall, and dressed in the costume the character wore in *The Empire Strikes Back*. He stood on the floor next to a display table. On the table itself were dozens of other *Star Wars* collectibles—action figures from the late 1970s, still in their original packages, a Darth Vader helmet, a complete stormtrooper uniform, a three-foot model of the Millennium Falcon.

"This is my pride and joy," said Dominic. He reached for a cylindrical tube that lay in a Lucite display case. "It's my Luke Skywalker Lightsaber." His eyes took on that unfocused look again, and he began swirling the tube in his hand as though its blade were lit and thrumming. "It's licensed by Lucasfilm. The only one. Lots of science fiction magazines have ads for lightsabers, and they're about one-third the price, but they're not *licensed,* see? Guys make 'em out in their garages, but they can't even call 'em lightsabers. They have to make up a different name for 'em. But this one is *licensed*, okay? It's got a certificate of authenticity, okay? This one is the *best*."

"You bought all this stuff?" asked Charles.

Dominic grinned. "Some I bought. Some I traded for." Then a strange smile flickered at the corner of his lips. "And some I got other ways."

Stolen. Of course. Probably lifted from comic book conventions across the country—the San Diego Comic-Con, the Chicago Con, Dragon*Con. Dominic's job at the studio, with its emphasis on technical knowledge, undoubtedly paid well. Here is where all the money went. A few dollars a week on junk food, a few on gas and utilities, and the rest lay on the shelves in this room.

That's how he lives, Charles thought. *He comes home from work, he plays with his high-tech gadgets, but for the most part he never leaves this room. Nothing else is real to him.*

"Dominic," said Charles, "we'd better hurry. My buyer for the artwork lives two hours away from here, and in two hours and fifteen minutes I want the deal to be *done*. Get it?" Charles had a flashing thought that he could grab Dominic's keys, walk out right now, and trundle off into the sunset in a 1977 Pinto that was missing on one cylinder. He held that vision for about a second before deciding that maybe an extra five minutes wouldn't hurt. Not only did Dominic understand the rat trap of a car well enough to keep it running—something Charles doubted *he* could do—he was also too unstable to be left unattended. There was no telling what the fool might do if Charles weren't around to stop him.

Dominic held up a bronze X-O Manowar ring, then a set of 1940s vintage Hyperman trading cards. Charles made a rolling, hurry-up gesture with his finger.

"Don't worry about the time, Charles," said Dominic, flipping a switch on the wall. "I've just activated my little warning system. We'll know when they get here."

Charles felt the blood drain from his face. "Warning system?" he said. "What for? When *who* gets here?"

Dominic did not even look at him. "Them," he said matter-of-factly. "Those kids who followed us." He reached for a bronze statuette of Psychoblade.

Charles shook his head. "No," he said. "That's not possible. Those kids are *dead!* Don't you understand? The guns went off. The video lab went up in flames. We killed them."

Dominic's eyes had taken on a glazed look. "No," he said, "they'll be here. They always escape from traps like that. They always find a way."

He slowly lifted his lightsaber and studied it. Charles groaned to himself at the slowness of the gesture. For Dominic, this was the careful handling of a museum piece; for Charles it was a waste of valuable time. But he said nothing. Two teenagers were dead, and the entire plan had taken on the tone of a funeral. Worse, Dominic was acting as though the funeral were his own—his and Charles's. He had insisted they come here before arranging the sale of the Hyperman art. A "last look," Dominic had called it. Charles didn't know why Dominic was being so fatalistic, but he went along with Dominic's whims. Dominic was unstable and temperamental, and Charles didn't want to pressure him any more than he had to.

"Who?" Charles demanded hoarsely. "Who always escapes?"

Dominic looked up at him. His lips tugged into a smile, and he let out a short, high-pitched giggle.

"The good guys," he said.

While Dominic examined his treasures, clutching some, caressing others, Charles drew a cell phone from his jacket pocket and punched in a number. The man who had agreed to distribute the Hyperman video had made a fortune dealing in high-end, comic-related collectibles. He had the wealth—and the lack of scruples—that Charles needed right now. The phone rang five, six, seven times before Charles pressed the end button and slammed down the wire antenna.

Dominic sat on the floor, holding a resin model of Godzilla. He let out a high-pitched *scree,* imitating the monster's cry.

"Dominic!" said Charles. "That's enough. Let's get out of here."

Just then a plastic box mounted on the wall began to flash red. It blinked in rhythm to a piercing siren, and a robotic voice began announcing, "Red alert…red alert…red alert…."

Dominic looked up at Charles, smiling. "They're **193** *heeere.*"

Charles slapped down the wall switch, shutting off the siren. In the silence that followed, he heard footsteps entering the room behind him.

"Don't tell me, let me guess," said a familiar voice. "You weren't expecting company, and it's the maid's day off."

Charles spun around and the cell phone dropped from his fingers, clattering against the floor. In the doorway, leaning casually—like a vamp from a 1940s crime film—stood the Sutter girl.

"Oh, don't let me interrupt business," she said. "Make your call. The sooner you can move the artwork, the sooner I'll have my cut."

Dominic eyed her, silent. The model lay in his lap, his hands gripping it protectively.

"I—I'm surprised to see you," said Charles warily. "Pleased, of course—but surprised."

She waved away his concern. "Accidents happen," she said. "And as you've already pointed out, I'm not exactly in a position to point fingers, am I?" She strolled into the room, gazing at the wealth of collectibles. "More to the point," she said, "you have my grandfather's artwork. You're obviously planning to sell it. I want my share."

Charles studied her, still unconvinced. "I thought this was a personal matter for you," he said. "I thought you were planning to return the artwork to your grandfather."

"My main concern," said Robin, sliding her finger along one of Dominic's shelves, checking it for dust, "is that my grandfather receives fair compensation for his work. You have a buyer who won't ask any questions. A sixty-year-old piece of cardboard won't buy my grandfather any luxuries. But fifty-thousand dollars *will*." She waited patiently for Charles's reply.

Charles decided he had to humor the girl. His only other option was to kill her…again.

"Well, then," he said, "since Dominic and I have the art, I suppose you'll have to be satisfied with *our* terms." He bent down and picked up the cell phone he had dropped. "I just tried calling my buyer. We'll have no problem getting our price, I'm sure." He grinned slyly. "He has substantial resources at his disposal—need I say more?"

The Sutter girl smiled. "No," she said. "My guess is, you've said enough."

Just then two men stepped into the room with guns drawn. Police badges dangled from leather holders at their belts.

One of the detectives spun Charles around and slapped a pair of handcuffs on his wrists. The second grabbed Dominic, who was still clutching his Godzilla model, and hoisted him to his feet. "Get the cell phone, Sam," he said. "We can use the redial button to track down their buyer." He handcuffed Dominic and gave the young man a push, guiding him out the door.

"Hey—*hey!*" said Dominic. "Don't step on Yoda."

epilogue

Four months later

Peter gazed up at the theater marquee, smiling not so much at the large letters screaming "Hyperman: the Movie," but at the smaller, more dignified letters underneath.

"Special appearance," he read aloud, "by Hyperman creator, Joe Sutter."

"Cool, huh?" said Jake.

Byte smiled but remained silent. Peter watched her study the marquee, nodding to herself. Mattie didn't speak either, gazing instead over the crowd of people or sneaking glances into the theater lobby.

Tonight was the premiere of the Hyperman movie. Since 10:00 A.M., fans had been gathering around the theater, spreading out blankets, cranking up boom boxes, and gobbling fast food in anticipation of the sold-out 8:00 P.M. showing. Their tickets guaranteed them a seat, but it was the excitement, the rumors whispered among the fans, the feeling of being part of an *event* that kept them from leaving and returning later. Most were also waiting for a chance to finally meet Joe Sutter, to shake his hand, to wish him well, to see his work again.

Peter pointed toward the lobby door, where Robin Sutter, dressed in a summer dress, her red hair trailing across her bare shoulders, was just exiting. She walked slowly, with clumsy, exaggerated care, in her high heels. "There she is," Peter said.

Robin's eyes swept over the crowd and located the Misfits. She walked over to them and, smiling briefly at Peter, sauntered past him and threw her arms around Byte. "Thanks," she whispered, "for helping to make this happen."

"I didn't do all this," said Byte. "I just kind of got the ball rolling."

Robin grinned slyly. "Before you refuse to take credit, you have to see the inside of the theater. It's amazing." Her smile broadened as she looked at all the Misfits. "Come on. I'll show you."

She led them to the lobby entrance, where a security guard nodded and stepped aside.

Hanging on the lobby walls, and scattered about on easels, were original Hyperman works by Joe Sutter. A few, like the painting Peter recognized from Sutter's living room, were large, bright works in acrylic or oil. Others were smaller works—pen-and-ink drawings, pastels, or watercolors. They filled the lobby, their bright colors shaming the slick movie posters at the entrance. Sutter himself, in suit and tie, sat at a table answering a reporter's questions, camera flashes exploding in his face.

"It gives me chills," Robin said. "In about half an hour, broadcast on national television, Hunter Brothers Studios is going to present Grandpa with his original artwork to *Hero Comics #1* and a check," she stood a little taller and affected a formal, public speaking voice, "'for his generous contribution to American culture.'"

"How big a check?" asked Mattie.

Byte gave him a light slap on the shoulder. "*Mattie!*"

Robin laughed. "Oh, please," she said. "It's hardly a secret. After all the sympathetic news coverage Grandpa's received in the last few months, the studio is doing cartwheels trying to look like good guys. The check is for one million dollars."

"Whew!" said Jake. "A million dollars sounds pretty good to me."

Robin shrugged. "They said the presentation would be great for ticket sales." She paused and looked around at the lobby and at the crowd waiting outside. "I guess," she said, "that sometimes it doesn't really matter why someone does a good deed, as long as it gets done."

She reached into her purse and withdrew a small box, gift-wrapped in Hyperman wrapping paper. "Byte," she said, "I ran into Janine Cook. She asked me to give you this."

Byte took the box, her face flushing as her friends stared at her, waiting for her to open it. She looked at each of them demurely, then ripped off the paper in a single violent tug. A small white cardboard box lay in her hand. She opened the box, lifted away a piece of cotton padding, and burst out in laughter.

"Rubber pointed ears!" she cried. "They're *perfect!*"

Mattie shrugged, unimpressed. "They're obsolete," he said. "Now everyone's going with big latex brow ridges if they want the alien look."

Ignoring the remark, Robin turned to Jake and Mattie. "Listen," she said, "it looks like Grandpa's finished talking to that reporter. He said he would bring some art board with him in case any of you guys wanted a sketch."

Jake and Mattie looked at each other, then raced to the table where her grandfather was seated. Peter, Byte, and Robin laughed for a moment, then fell silent. After a moment, Byte blushed and made a vague, waving gesture toward Joe Sutter's table.

"So," she said, "I guess I'll ask…uh…ask for a sketch, too. I mean, I haven't always been a huge comic fan or anything, but—well, I do like your grandpa's stuff, don't get me wrong." She paused and wrinkled her nose, grinning goofily. "I mean…."

Finally she shrugged.

"Oh, forget it," she said. "I'm leaving so you two can talk." She walked off to look at the gallery, leaving Peter and Robin alone.

"Hmmm," said Peter, "why do I feel as though I've just been set up?"

Robin smiled at him, that familiar eyebrow cocked. "Maybe you have."

Peter smiled back. "It's weird not having spoken with you in so long—new semester, new classes, finals and everything. How are you doing?"

"Well, you know the charges against me were dropped," she said. "Actually, the police were happiest to get hold of Dominic. Turns out half the collectibles in the guy's bedroom had been reported stolen at one time or another. He and his friend Charles Leach will spend the next five or so years in jail."

"No," said Peter. "I know all that stuff. I was asking about *you*."

Robin turned and gazed at her grandfather, who was chatting with Jake, Mattie, and Byte. "Oh, I'm just great," she said. "But you know who's really changed through all this, Peter? Grandpa. It's like he's become a different person. It's not the money—though he deserves at least that. It's the recognition, the appreciation for his work. I can't tell you how many people have contacted him. They don't ask for anything; they just send these long, handwritten letters relating childhood memories about Hyperman, or telling funny stories. It's meant everything to him."

Peter wasn't certain how to respond, and he realized suddenly that—yet again—Robin Sutter had left him temporarily speechless. He let his eyes wander over the lobby—at the paintings, at the huge Hyperman movie posters, at the film executives in their suits, at Joe Sutter bent over his sketch pad, pen darting furiously.

"Grandpa and Dad were really angry with me," she said. "I think they understand my motives, though they haven't completely forgiven me yet. Dad says that sometime after I'm married and have my third or fourth child I won't be grounded anymore." She smiled.

"I've been wanting to tell you something," Peter said finally. "You've been really great all through this—well, with some minor exceptions I'm willing to forget. What I'm saying is, if you wanted, you know, to be an official member of the group—" Peter reached into his pocket and withdrew a business card. He handed it to Robin.

misfits inc.
investigations

Mysteries are no mystery to us!

Jake Armstrong
Peter Braddock

Matthew Ramiro
Byte Salzmann

Robin studied the card. "You mean you guys do this kind of stuff all the time?" she asked, teasing. "Solve crimes? Get shot at? Wreak destruction on poor, unsuspecting movie studios?" She thought a moment. "I guess the last part was my fault."

Peter laughed. "Well, we needed after-school jobs, and McDonald's wasn't hiring." He looked down at the floor, his finger pressed thoughtfully against the nose bridge of his glasses. Peter could feel a warmth as his face reddened, so he kept his face down and his eyes on the ground until the sensation passed. Then he looked up again at Robin. "It's not just about solving mysteries. It's about having good friends. The mysteries just sort of…*find* us."

"Thanks," Robin said. "I'll keep the offer in mind, but I think, for now at least, I'd better pass. My father's keeping a close eye on me for a while. But it's not just that." She turned to look at her grandfather. "He's an old man, Peter. And all of a sudden he's nothing like the grandfather I've known all my life. I think I'd really regret it if I didn't take the time to get to know him." She shook her head, laughing. "You know what he did? Yesterday he insisted I go with him to the animal shelter because he wanted me to help him pick out a *puppy*. For years he's hidden in that house, drowning himself in old movies, and now he wants a squirming, yapping, cuddly puppy—can you imagine?"

Robin stood a little closer to Peter and let her hand brush his. Their fingers touched almost accidentally, then interlocked for a moment.

"See you around, Braddock," she said, pulling away. She smiled, then she stepped off into the crowd of guests.

At first Peter felt a twinge as he watched her go, but this was followed by an unexpected sense of relief. The feeling of being torn, of being pulled in two different directions, left him. Peter turned to look at Byte. She was gazing at a sketch Joe Sutter had drawn for Mattie. Somehow she must have felt Peter's eyes on her because she looked up, smiled, and gave him a little wave.

He wandered over to the gallery of art and stood in front of a huge acrylic painting of Hyperman. Though newly painted, the image was very familiar to him: the hero, poised in the sky, cape whipping behind him as he gazed down protectively on the city below. Peter thought back to when he was seven, a bright yellow towel wrapped around his neck as he leaped from a fence-post—a child with a comic book rolled into his back pocket, a child who worshipped a hero and dreamed he could fly.